Family Crimes

Ellie McLellan Genealogy Mystery - Book 4

Beth Farrar

This is a work of fiction. Any references to real people or places are used fictitiously; other names and places are products of the author's imagination. Any resemblance to actual people or places is entirely coincidental, except for Montreal – that's real!

Edited by Ronnie Pelletier

Cover by GetCovers.com

First edition published – 2023

eBook ISBN: 978-1-7386664-9-2

Paperback ISBN: 978-1-7380125-0-3

Hardcover ISBN: 978-1-7380125-1-0

No part of this book was written by AI – just a human's blood, sweat and tears (and some stress!).

Author's Note: Being a Canadian author, please excuse any double "l"s or wayward "u"s in words, eh. Please do not flag them. Much appreciated.

Also By

Ellie McLellan Genealogy Mystery Series

Family Secrets – Book 1

Family Mistakes – Book 2

Family Promises – Book 3

Sign up for my newsletter at bethfarrar.com!

Contents

When you believe in yourself, and have a great support network, there's nothing you can't achieve.

My family has been there for me through all the ups and downs of this amazing publishing journey.

You guys are vunderbar!

Chapter One

"I can't believe I got stuck behind a school bus!" Ellie said as she raced into the back room of the Cozy Corner Café for her Wednesday morning meeting with her senior's genealogy group. "Where has the summer gone?" she asked as she took off her jean jacket and hung it on the back of a chair.

"I felt it the minute I woke up," Ruth Cotter said from her seat beside her beau, Jeremy Butler. "Even though it's been decades since I taught, there's something exciting about the first day of school."

Jeremy took her hand and gave it a squeeze. "Ruth was up rather early today. She called at five for our morning chat!"

"Go on with you," Ruth's older sister, Shirley, said from across the table. "None of us sleeps normally at our age. And Jeremy, you were already awake too." One glance at the sisters and anyone could tell they were related, but Ruth was tiny while Shirley was a stout woman. They both shared their mother's smile.

"And we've all gotten used to sleeping when we can," Phil Richards said. "We're all eighty-seven or older, except for the spring chicken."

"Oh, Phil." Ellie's Aunt Norma gave him a wink. "You say the nicest things." Norma loved to tease Phil, and now that he knew she meant it in fun, he didn't always blush at the comments Norma made. He had even taken to predicting which of her science fiction shirts she would wear at their meetings. Today was a Star Wars Wookie shirt, along with a red checkered lumberjack sweater and blue pants. At least she wasn't wearing her beloved orange crocs.

"Well, I for one never minded my kids going back to school," Doreen Hastings said, her knitting needles clacking away. "Love them though I did, when they started out on their own lives, it was a relief to have time to myself. They got into all kinds of scrapes when they were young. Thank goodness for my knitting." She held up her needles. "It kept me sane!"

"Still does, I would assume?" Norma asked. She envied Doreen's dedication, or addiction, to her hobby. It kept her mind and hands occupied.

When Doreen held up her latest creation and Phil opened his mouth to comment, but remained silent, Shirley asked his question for him. "And what are you making this time, Doreen? That's not a scarf, is it?"

"No." Doreen held up a lumpy bundle in cascading colors. "I found this amazing wool and decided to try my hand at a hat."

There were nods all around, though no one was sure what the final product would turn out to be. While Doreen had been knitting most of her life, she had never made much beyond scarves, or long strips she sewed together to make blankets. They were all recipients of one of her bright winter scarves.

Ellie brushed a strand of wind-blown brown hair from her face and put her laptop on the table. "I'm thrilled we've agreed to come in the mornings from now on. This should work out well for all of us."

"Like I said." Shirley nodded around at her friends. "We've all been up for hours."

"And I don't mind heading to bed early," Tess said. Her husband, Lennie, nodded in agreement, stifling a yawn behind his hand.

The Seniors Genealogy Group had been meeting at the Cozy Corner Café for over a year. Its main purpose had been for Ellie to teach them how to write their own life stories. Her experience as a genealogist had helped certain members solve family mysteries, and she had become quite fond of the group. With an average age of ninety, some older, some younger by mere years, Ellie had not only shared her skills, but learned a lot about life from them in return. The meetings were not only educational, but social, and they had formed a tight group.

"So," Ellie said, "I was thinking about doing something a little different today. Even though we're writing our own personal stories, or memoirs, we should acknowledge other people who had a part in our lives." She looked at their captivated faces. "So, let's talk about crime. Did you ever commit a crime or get arrested? Or do you know of any family members who have, or maybe we can search for some that we never knew about."

"Well!" Phil let out a breath and looked everywhere but at his fellow seniors.

Norma fidgeted in her seat and paid unusual attention to her nails.

"I wasn't a criminal lawyer," Lennie said, "but I've seen many people in trouble in my day."

"I got a speeding ticket," Tess said in a small voice.

Lennie turned to her with a frown. "When was this?"

"Oh." Tess made a face, as if searching for the answer. "It was shortly after David started kindergarten. I was late to pick him up at school and I..." She shrugged her shoulders.

"You never told me that," Lennie said.

"It wasn't a big thing," Tess said. She picked at an invisible piece of fluff on her dark blue pants. "Just a little ticket. I paid it right away and I never got another one after that."

Ellie watched the couple, unsure how Lennie would react. He had joined the group to support his wife, and everyone had become used to his grumpiness. But today he surprised them all.

"I got one too," he grinned at her. "When you went into labour with David, I had to get home as fast as I could to pick you up to get to the hospital. Remember how frazzled I was when I walked in?"

"I do." Tess nodded. "I was more worried about you than about having a baby!"

"I explained everything to the officer, and while he was sympathetic, he wrote the ticket fast and congratulated me."

"You mean you didn't get off for a very noble reason?" Shirley asked.

"Nor should I have," Lennie said. "It turned out okay in the end."

"Is David aware that he caused all your criminal activity?" Ruth joked.

"He will be." Lennie gave Tess a wink.

Daphne, second in command at the Cozy Corner Café, placed a tray of cups on the table. "Maggie's at her grandmother's cabin, but she'll be back tomorrow. Until then, I'm in charge." She blew a strand of hair from her eyes and nodded at them all. "Snackscoming up." She returned with a plate of chocolate chip cookies and a large pot of tea. She poured for everyone and then returned to the counter to serve a couple who had just entered.

"I never thought Maggie would leave this place," Shirley said.

"She didn't leave," Ellie said. "She needed a break. She's had the Café for two years now, and she's hardly taken any time for herself that whole time."

"And it's certainly not a crime to look after yourself!" Doreen said.

"Speaking of which," Ellie said, "does anyone have any stories, or should we see who we can find online?" She opened her laptop and looked around, waiting for someone to offer their own tales of wrong doing.

"How would we find a criminal in our family if no one ever talked about it?" Doreen asked, lowering her needles and reaching for a cookie.

"That's a good question," Ellie said. "Without a name and date, it might be difficult to locate that information. What you could do is start with a general Google search and..."

As a group, the seniors all held up a hand and said "And Google is our friend," then burst out laughing.

"I say that a lot, don't I?" Ellie smiled at them. "But it's true. And while Ancestry does have a ton of records regarding crimes and criminals, it helps to narrow things down as best you can. Does anyone have an ancestor they want to use as an example?"

A silence fell over them, and then Phil shifted in his seat. "My grandfather came from England around 1895 or so. My father was under the impression that he *had* to leave, and I've always wondered about that. He wasn't the easiest man to get to know. He died when I was ten."

"What was his name and whereabouts in England did he live?" Ellie asked, fingers poised above her keyboard.

"His name was Walter Samuel Richard and he lived in London."

"Oh." Ellie perked up. "He might be in the Old Bailey records." She typed furiously and her eyes widened in surprise. "Phil, there's something here." She turned the laptop around so they could all see the screen. "This is what the site looks like. I'll read out bits of it. Let me see." She swung it back towards herself.

"Wait!" Shirley exclaimed. "How can we be sure this is his grandfather?"

"That's another good question," Ellie said with an approving nod. "As you saw," she angled herself towards the screen and pointed to the list, "there is only one person with that full name. And it has his year of birth. Hang on." She swung the laptop around and typed again. "I've now removed the Samuel and you see three other Walter Richard names appearing. One has a year of birth and the others don't. The records show that Walter Samuel Richard was being prosecuted, which is why he is noted as a defendant. So, it would stand to reason that if he were a witness, victim or judiciary, there wouldn't be much of a reason for him to leave the country."

Phil sat still, hands clenched, as if the event that occurred decades ago could have some bearing on his current life. "But Dad said he *did* have to leave. So, I'll agree with you there, Ellie."

She returned to the entry. "So, they caught him for burglary. Phil, I'll let you read this all yourself later, but it gives a transcribed version of the actual court hearing, with witnesses and all, then the verdict."

"Which was?" Phil asked.

"Guilty."

Shirley leaned forward in keen interest. "What was his sentence?"

"Three years' penal servitude."

"Which means?"

"Hang on." Ellie opened another tab and scanned the page. "So, penal servitude became a replacement for transportation and was introduced in 1853. It meant hard labour in a convict prison."

"Harsh," Tess muttered. "Just for burglary."

"Those were tough times," Phil said. "I can only imagine what that would have entailed for my grandfather. He wasn't a big man, and perhaps four years of hard labour did him some damage."

"And no one ever spoke about it?" Lennie asked him.

"Never heard a whisper," Phil said. "But something wasn't right, and my dad was always curious. He asked my Grandad once, right in front of us, why he had left England. My Grandad got furious. It was all very cryptic at the time between the adults, but now I understand why he wouldn't have wanted to stay there."

Shirley leaned over and took a cookie. "How do you feel about this, Phil?"

"I have convict blood in my veins!" Phil raised an eyebrow at her, trying to lighten the mood. "Who's next?"

Ellie held up a cookie and counted the number of chocolate chips on it. One of her biggest weaknesses was chocolate, and Maggie's baking drew her like a bee to honey. "You should all take some time and look through Ancestry's criminal record base. There are records from all over the world. But be warned, you could lose hours diving down rabbit holes of people who aren't even your ancestors!"

They dug into the cookies until the plate was empty, and finished their tea before settling back into the topic of the day.

"Oh," said Tess, "don't forget I found my grandfather had been in prison through the census records."

"Which we had an inkling of through a newspaper article," Ellie reminded her. "You can search Ancestry, NARA and Find My Past, among others, for records like this."

"And I guess I should be lucky they didn't transport my grandfather to another country," Phil said. "I'm glad he came to Canada. Though Australia looks interesting as well."

"Fun fact," Ellie said, wiping her fingers on a napkin and eyeing the last cookie on Norma's plate. She told herself to be strong and look away. "England started shipping criminals to the US in the 1700s. Some of those poor people had sentences that lasted up to fourteen years."

"You mean they were indentured servants?" Doreen stopped to gaze up at Ellie in shock before quickly catching a loose stitch on her needle.

"Exactly. And the UK National Archives even have pictures of criminals. And Phil, that Old Bailey record for your grandfather? I saved it because you might want to check out the original copy of the court case. It's quite fascinating. So, it doesn't matter where you live, most countries have some sort of records available to search. But you might need to know the location the event happened, or the judicial court nearest to the event."

"Can we switch gears for one second?" Tess asked.

"Sure thing," Ellie said.

"How would I go about finding where my grandfather is buried? No one has that information, and I've been on the phone the past week to any relative who might have a clue."

"Oh, I know this one!" Ruth said. "I was looking through a site called Find a Grave and, Shirley, I found Aunt Alma's resting place."

"Now that is interesting," Shirley said. She looked around the table and let the tension build. "Aunt Alma had fourteen children and one day she up and left her whole family. We never heard from her again. We all presumed she had died."

"She did," Ruth said. "But in Vancouver. In 1952. So, about two years after she left."

"But what if we don't have the name of the cemetery?" Tess asked.

"Let's open the site and see what we can find." Ellie typed in the site location and once again swung the laptop around so everyone could see. "So, you put the person's name in a region where you think they might be buried, birth date and death date. I'll type in your grandfather's name, and what was the year he died?"

"Edward Halbert," Tess said. "And we know that he died in Hawk Station, Ontario in 1920".

"Which is Dunlop County," Ellie said, focusing on entering the information. "And voila! There is an Edward Halbert buried in Lakeview Cemetery, died 1920. Let's open it up."

"It says he was born in 1881 in Regina. And look, there's a picture of his tombstone!" Tess said excitedly, pointing to the screen.

"What's that on the right-hand side?" Lennie asked. "Records on Ancestry?"

"Those are hints that may be related to your grandfather, and it looks like there's a marriage record and a census return," Ellie answered, her focus glued to the screen.

"Can we see the marriage record?" Tess asked.

When Ellie opened it and showed the group, Tess sat back with a frown. "This is for his second marriage, right? Because that's not my grandmother's name!"

"Let me screenshot it for you so you can study it later," Ellie said as she saved the page for Tess.

With his chin in his hand, Phil leaned on the table, staring at the screen. "So, what you're saying is we can go to this site for free and search for anyone?"

"Yes," Ellie said. "If you wanted to see any of the Ancestry links, however, you'd need a membership to Ancestry."

"Wait a minute," Doreen said. "How did Find a Grave get all this information in the first place? Where did it come from?"

"Anyone can add information and pictures to the site." Ellie turned the laptop back towards her and popped in a USB stick to download the marriage certificate for Tess.

"But how can you be sure what's written there is real?" Phil asked, sitting back with his arms crossed now, not looking too sure of this whole idea.

"It's put together by genealogists and volunteers." Ellie passed the stick to Tess, who nodded her thanks. "I know of a few people who plan their vacations around visiting out of the way cemeteries and documenting all the information they can. It's quite fun!"

"Are you a few people?" Norma teased.

"One of many," Ellie said.

"Ellie." Norma glanced down at her nails. She hesitated, then shook her head as if coming to a decision. "Do you remember Uncle Tommy?"

Ellie took a minute and then nodded. "I do. Mom and Dad never wanted him to come in the house. I never understood. He seemed like a nice guy."

"That's because he *was* a very kind man. And a kleptomaniac. I helped him get away with stealing a lot of jewelry."

Chapter Two

"You've just admitted to something very serious," Lennie said slowly. "And there's no statute of limitations for that type of crime in Canada."

"This is nonsense!" Ellie sputtered. "You'd never do such a thing, Aunt Norma!"

Norma shifted in her seat, trying to get comfortable. She was about to share her secret, and it felt almost freeing. But the acid burn in the pit of her stomach was not pleasant.

"You don't have to say anymore," Lennie cautioned her. Being a retired lawyer never stopped him from giving advice.

"I was ten years old," Norma said.

"Surely, she can't be held as an accessory after all this time," Tess said loudly, as if the mere tone of her voice would make it so.

"Maybe you should tell us the entire story," Ruth suggested.

"Right after my tenth birthday," Norma started, "my family took a holiday to our usual vacation spot."

"Virginia's Cabins?" Ellie asked in surprise.

"The very place."

"Did my dad go too?"

Norma nodded. "He was about five at the time." She gave herself a minute to gather her thoughts. "So, anyway, our week there was almost over when Uncle Tommy turned up. He hadn't planned on being there, but said he was passing through on his way to a job, and would stay for only one night. The owners found him a spot to sleep and that was that."

"Virginia's Cabins rings a bell," Phil said. "That's about two hours north of here, right?"

"On Lake Samson, yes," Norma said.

"I've wanted to visit there. It looks quite nice." He settled back in his seat, arms still crossed, waiting for her to continue her tale.

"We'd been going there for years, but that was the last time we ever went." Norma shifted around in her chair. Telling this story was harder than she thought it would be. But now was the time to let it all out and she hoped she'd feel better for it. "I made sure we never went back."

"What happened?" Ellie asked.

"As I mentioned, Tommy suffered from kleptomania." Norma looked at her fellow seniors. "Not his fault. Tommy's behavior was caused by a mental health condition, and he had been diagnosed when he was younger. We always kept our eyes on him when he was around, though, because things tended to disappear."

"What did he steal from the cabins?" Shirley asked.

"I saw him coming out of the owner's cabin when everyone was down at the docks for afternoon games, and he was moving fast. He disappeared into his own little cabin. Some people would consider it just a shed, but they'd set it up as an overflow sleeping spot for families. He came out minutes later, empty-handed, and headed down to the beach as if nothing had happened."

"How can you be sure he stole something?" Doreen asked, all attempts at knitting forgotten as she was drawn into the story.

"Because I ran into his cabin right after and found a bag of jewelry. There were some marvelous pieces in there, and most seemed quite valuable."

"What did you do?" Tess asked, wide eyed.

"I buried the bag."

They all fell silent, taking in this piece of information.

"But why didn't you just give it back?" Ruth asked.

"Because she'd have to explain how she had it, and that would implicate her as the thief, or she would have to tell on Tommy," Lennie explained patiently, understanding the situation Norma had found herself in.

"You could have left it on their kitchen table and taken off," Shirley said.

"I was ten and I was scared. I didn't think of that," Norma admitted. "And Tommy was a lovely man, except for his illness. And he was *all* I was thinking about. He'd been caught before and let off because of his condition, but warned he would go to jail if it continued. I mean, he was in therapy and all, and that was a huge thing in those days. It was like a brand of something seriously wrong with you. And he tried, he really did, but he couldn't resist."

Ellie continued her typing. "The Mayo Clinic site says kleptomania is a disorder that makes people steal things they don't even need. It's an impulse control disorder."

"Exactly," Norma nodded. "And he never planned to steal things. Something would come over him at these times, and he couldn't help himself."

"Poor man," Tess said.

"So, here I was, ten years old, a bag of jewelry in my hands and an uncle who would end up in jail if his crime were to be discovered." Norma shrugged. "I did the first thing that came to mind. I found a shovel from behind a shed, dug a hole in the ground under some tree roots, and buried it all."

"Did they notice the jewelry missing?" Lennie asked, always one to go straight to the facts.

"They did." Norma sighed. "He'd left the jewelry box askew, and the woman noticed it right away. She came thundering out, yelling for her husband. Everyone gathered around and her husband made a big to do about calling the police."

"Surely, Tommy would have given them back," Jeremy said.

"He didn't have them anymore," Norma reminded him. "And he didn't say a word. It was as if he had no memory of having taken anything! And that's when I became an accomplice. I said nothing as well."

"Sweet Marie!" Shirley said. "So, what happened to the buried treasure?"

"Nothing," Norma said. "We left that afternoon, and I wanted nothing more to do with it. I've thought about it over the years, but never wanted to bring it all up again. Tommy died years ago, but I've been afraid of what still might happen."

"To you?" Ellie asked.

"Yes," Norma mumbled. "I'm more of a coward than I thought. Could I go to jail?"

"I don't think so," Lennie said. "But I'm not sure about this whole scenario."

Again, Ellie returned to her laptop. "Okay. So, here's the exact wording of the Criminal Code, Article 23(1). "An accessory after the fact to an offence is one who, knowing that a person has been a party to the offence, receives, comforts or assists that person for the purpose of enabling that person to escape."

"Right," Lennie said. "So, you did not receive, comfort, or assist that person for the purpose of enabling that person to escape, did you?"

"No. But I knew what he had done, and I took the goods myself and buried them!" Norma's voice rose and two bright spots appeared on her cheeks. "Technically, I was stealing them, too!"

"Not necessarily," Lennie said, holding up a hand. "There's a lot to be considered here. You were ten years old, for goodness' sake! We'll have to look into that."

"Why not just go back, dig them up, and return them now?" Shirley asked.

They all turned to her, surprised by her logical suggestion.

Norma froze. The idea of returning to the scene of the crime sent a shiver through her body. "But I'd never remember where I buried them, and who would I return them to? It's been so long."

"I bet there's a relative somewhere who'd be thrilled to have the items back, and hear the story," Jeremey said. "I doubt anyone would press charges at this late date!"

"The owners had a daughter. Virginia," Norma said, as if lost in thoughts of the vacation in question. "She was younger than me, always followed me around. She played the flute. Nice kid."

"And I bet once you're there, you could find the location," Phil added, sitting forward, thoroughly engaged in the crime at hand.

"Why don't we all go and see what we can find?" Jeremy suggested.

"You mean like a vacation?" Ruth asked.

"It's only what—two hours away?" Jeremy asked. "Why not?"

"Road trip!" Ellie grinned. Road trips were right up there with chocolate as some of her favorite things.

"Let's go on a mini-vacation," Jeremy said. "Stay for a night and maybe solve a crime at the same time."

"Oh, I don't know..." Norma hemmed and hawed, not liking this one bit.

"This would be a perfect time to go," Phil said. "Everything's cheaper off season, and we're all seniors. Imagine the discounts we'll get!"

The others agreed, excited at the prospect of getting away for some detective work.

"Okay." Ellie stood up, signaling the end of the meeting. "Let's meet again to plan. When?"

"Tomorrow!" Phil said. "We'll sort things through and nail down this adventure."

They all nodded their agreement and chatted excitedly as they made their way out of the Café and off to their respective homes. Except for Norma. She was the last one out. She stood in the parking lot, lost in thought, unsure that digging up the past would be a good idea for anyone.

Chapter Three

"Ellie?" The deep Scottish accent of her boyfriend, Quinn, reached her from the ground floor of her farmhouse. She was, at the moment, inside the secret playroom that had lain hidden behind the closet of what used to be her late daughter's room.

"Ellie?" The voice was closer.

"In here," she called to him, as she shimmied out of the hole and stood up in the bedroom closet, screwdriver in one hand, brushing cobwebs from her hair with the other.

Quinn's broad shoulders filled the doorway. "What are you doing?"

She held up the screwdriver. "Ruth and Shirley told me about their old playroom. Their father built it behind their bedroom, through the closet, and I wanted to see what it looks like. I never got around to it before, but I've got the door open. Here, come with me."

And with that, she disappeared into the hole and was gone.

Quinn moved closer, but didn't follow her. A fine bead of sweat formed on his upper lip.

Ellie's head popped out of the small opening at the back of the closet. She grinned like a child at Christmas. "Come on in! It's amazing in here." She motioned behind her with her flashlight and crawled further into the dark space beyond.

But still, he didn't move.

He could see the beam of light bouncing off the walls within, took a deep breath, bent down and squeezed his large frame through the tight opening.

"Would you look at this!" Ellie sat cross-legged on the floor by the furthest wall. A glimmer of sunlight shone through a grimy window near the ceiling, but it cast the rest of the room in a grey gloom. Ellie's flashlight kept bouncing from one spot to another, highlighting toys, a small table and chairs, and a bookcase. "I still remember when Ruth and Shirley sold this farm to Adam and me. It was a dream come true. I've loved this property and farmhouse since the moment I first rode past it on my bike. But I never knew about this room."

Quinn lowered himself to the floor, one hand gripping the opening, the other clenched beside his leg. Sweat trickled down his back. "Sorry, what is this place again?"

"I told you," Ellie kept glancing around, never once focusing on him. "Ruth and Shirley used this as a play area. I wish I had known about it when Winnie was alive. She could have had a great time in here. We'd even have put electricity in for her. I'm surprised it's so dry and warmish. But the dust is a bit much!"

Quinn's silence finally drew her attention, and she shifted to his side. "What's wrong? You look horrible." She accidentally flashed him full in the face with the light and he pushed it aside, turning his head away. "Sorry!"

"Yeah, I'm not a fan of – of closed up spaces," he stammered. "Got locked in a cupboard once as a child during a hide and seek game. They couldn't get me out for almost thirty minutes. They had to take the door off."

"I'm sorry." She shuffled back. "You don't have to stay in here, Quinn. I'll be out in a minute."

"No, no." He wiped his forehead with his shirt sleeve and forced himself to release his death grip on the doorframe. "Tell me what you've found."

Ellie took another worried glance at him, then aimed the flashlight around the room, showing him the riches that had been left behind. "Toys for girls, but this is interesting." She handed him an old newspaper, the dust flaking off as it passed from hand-to-hand. "Check out the date and the heading."

"September 4, 1939, French Attack on Western Front."

"Britain had declared war against the Germans on September 3rd. Canada declared they would join the fighting on September 10th. Can you imagine how scary that was for Ruth and Shirley?" Ellie sat back on the floor with a thud, thoughts of what her friends had lived through during those years too unsettling to think about.

"They must have been quite young then," Quinn said. He wiped the sweat on his upper lip, and Ellie stood up.

"Okay," she shooed him towards the door. "Out we go. I shouldn't have kept you here."

Quinn got up in a rush, only to bend back down to squeeze through the opening and into the sunshine and fresh air of the bedroom.

"I'll be right with you!" Ellie turned back, grabbed a book from the bookshelf, then joined him in the room. She handed him the book and returned to the business of closing up the entrance to the secret playroom.

"What's this?"

She took it from him, dusted off the cover as best she could, and revealed it. The book had obviously been read many times, as its cover was worn and the spine loose. "Madeline. It was a favorite of mine, and I see it was Ruth's too. She told me Shirley hated going in that room, so I'm guessing most of the things there belonged to Ruth. I want to clean the book up and return it to her."

As Quinn followed Ellie back to the kitchen, they were welcomed by her golden-brown Labrador, Cali. "The group is going on a mini-vacation," she said, washing up quickly in the kitchen sink before pulling sandwich meats and bread from the refrigerator for lunch.

"And when is this to happen?" Quinn leaned against the counter and watched her excitement build. Cali sat at his feet, loving the deep head rub Quinn was giving her.

“We’re meeting tomorrow morning to make the arrangements.” Ellie slapped together two huge sandwiches, knowing that what she didn’t finish, Quinn would gladly help her with.

“Where are you planning to go?” He carried the food to the table while she got them drinks. He motioned for Cali to go lie down. She found a wayward toy by the stove, grabbed it and went to her spot by the door. Since Quinn had started renting the barn for his furniture business, and living in Ellie’s spare room, Cali had accepted him as part of the family. And most days she followed him like a shadow.

“It’s quite the story, actually,” Ellie said, sitting at the table with him. “We were talking about family criminals or crimes in general and Aunt Norma told us a tale about my Uncle Tommy being a kleptomaniac.” She took a small bite, chewed quickly, and continued, “He was a lovely man, but he had this problem. My parents didn’t like him in the house, and it all makes sense now.”

“What did this Uncle Tommy do that is causing this adventure?” Quinn loved watching the twinkle in her eyes when she was engaged in a mystery.

“Well.” Ellie put her sandwich down and leaned forward. “While on vacation, Aunt Norma saw him steal a bag of jewelry from the owners of the campground. It’s not really a campground, it’s more a cabin ground, and it’s where the family used to go for their annual vacations.”

“How old was she?”

“Ten,” Ellie said. “She knew that Uncle Tommy would be in big trouble, possibly even get some jail time, if they found him with the items. So, she took them from his cabin and buried them!”

Quinn sat back in surprise. “She did that at ten years old?”

“Aunt Norma has always been ... unique.” Ellie picked up her sandwich again. “She’s very knowledgeable and adaptive.”

“So, what happened to the stolen goods?”

“Nothing.” Ellie took another small bite. “They’re still there.”

"Wait." Quinn frowned. "Are you telling me that this trip back there is to dig up said stolen goods?"

"Exactly!" Ellie's grin was contagious.

"What if they're not there?"

"Then they're not there." Ellie wiped her mouth with her napkin. "But Aunt Norma has had this heavy weight hanging over her. She's afraid to find the jewelry and end up going to jail, but I think part of her wants to see if she can return them. Apparently, there was a daughter of the owners who used to play with Norma."

"I doubt your aunt would be in any trouble," Quinn said, "but I'm not up on Canadian law."

Ellie hopped up and gathered their dishes, placing them in the sink for a later clean up.

"Can I sit in on the meeting tomorrow?" Quinn asked, pushing his chair in under the table and reaching for her hand.

"Professional curiosity?" Ellie joked.

"I am curious, that's a fact." Quinn pulled her close for a hug. "But I don't have any rush jobs at the moment, and I could do with a break."

Ellie pulled back and looked at the face she had come to love. The scar that ran from his temple to his jaw had become as beloved as his blue eyes. "I think the group would be delighted to see you."

"Sounds like a plan." Quinn kissed her quick and then headed for the door, Cali by his side.

***

Norma's home was quaint, two bedrooms, one of which was an office, living room, kitchen and good-sized bathroom—she liked to soak in the claw-foot bathtub. When she returned from the unsettling genealogy meeting, lunch was the furthest thing from her mind. Instead, she hurried to her office and searched out her old family scrapbooks.

She found them on the highest shelf in the closet, of course. But being a spry seventy-three years young, she managed to get them down with the help of a step stool and concentration. The one she was searching for was on the top and relatively slim.

Taking it to the living room, she sank into her deep cushioned favorite chair and spread the scrapbook across her lap. Opening it to the first page, she marvelled at how much effort her mother had put into creating these capsules of memory for the family. Each trip was presented in a series of photos, chronically the journey from start to finish. In those days, cameras used film, and Norma knew a lot of those pictures had been ruined, mostly because of the antics of her and her siblings goofing around in front of the lens. But her mother never made a fuss; just went about documenting their adventures.

Norma flipped through the pages and stopped at the specific vacation she was looking for. Virginia's Cabins, one of the hottest Augusts on record. The first picture was of the family all piled in the car, except for mom, who was behind the camera. Norma turned the pages quickly, only noticing now that there were only two pictures of her mother for the whole vacation. One of her parents with their arms around each other on the dock, mom holding up a fishing rod with a fish. The only fish she had ever caught, and one she had steadfastly refused to remove from the line.

And the other photo was of her mom sitting by herself on the front porch of the cabin, the sunset in the distance, a smile on her face and her eyes closed. Norma remembered this photo in particular because she had taken it herself. She'd snuck the camera off the kitchen table and walked off as her mom was having a break. Norma hid behind some trees and looked back at her mom, framed the shot as best she could, and clicked. Her mom had been so surprised when this was one of the better pictures from that roll of film. And it had always been one of Norma's favorites.

Turning back to the first picture of that vacation, Norma took the time to look at her siblings' grinning faces, and her father's resigned stare, the sweat beading on his forehead. It had been a glorious holiday. At least, until the last day.

Finding the last picture of the trip, the one her mom always required a fellow vacationer to take for her, showed her parents leaning against each other, somewhat rested, the kids all sun burnt and positioned around them. And then Norma. She stood off from her siblings, a fake smile on her face, her eyes worried and sad.

It took Norma ten minutes to look through the rest of the pictures. She was searching for someone in particular, and she found her. The owner's daughter was in the background of one photograph of Norma and her brother, while Ellie's dad threw bean bags at a box. The girl had blond hair in pigtails, glasses, and always wore overall shorts.

Norma smiled as the memories came flooding back. Snippets of remembrances of Virginia. Norma wondered if she was still alive and what her life was like. Virginia had been musically gifted, playing the flute at a young age, and sometimes filling the whole cabin area with beautiful music.

But what Norma remembered most was how Virginia was always around, watching. No matter how often Norma invited the girl to join in their games, Virginia would always shake her head and move away.

When she finally closed the scrapbook, Norma had made her decision. She'd do this. She'd go back to Virginia's Cabins and look for the stolen jewelry. But if she didn't do it soon, she never would. And if she could, perhaps with her group's help, she'd find out if Virginia was still alive and return it all to her. Surely, the mature Virginia wouldn't want to press charges against her, would she?

Chapter Four

"So, I'm afraid we won't be able to join you," Tess told the group the next morning at the Cozy Corner Café as Ellie and Quinn strode in. "But you'll have to fill us in when you get back."

"Sorry all, but I'm out as well," Doreen said, her knitting still in its bag on the floor by her feet. "I'm heading out to visit my daughter tomorrow, though I wish I could reschedule."

"How exciting," Tess said. "I bet you'll have a great time with the grandkids."

"Better than our doctors' appointments, that's for sure," grumbled Lennie.

"Did you pick a date already?" Ellie asked in surprise.

"I hope you don't mind, but I got in touch with the owners of the cabins last night," Norma said. "There's a one-night stay, but it's tomorrow. We'll be alone while we're there, but they're booked solid after that until closing."

"Good to see you, Quinn," Ruth smiled at him. "Taking a break?"

"I wanted to hear all about your coming adventure." He sat beside Ruth, kissed her on the cheek, and nodded hello to everyone else. "And ask if you wouldn't mind if I join you on your trip."

"Oh, what fun," Norma said, sending Ellie a knowing look.

Ellie ignored her aunt and busied herself by pulling a parcel wrapped in flowered paper and ribbons from her bag. She handed it to Ruth.

"What's this?" Ruth asked in surprise. "It's not my birthday!" But she peeled the paper back as carefully as possible until the gift was revealed. She held it up for all to see. "Oh, Ellie, you've been in the room, haven't you?"

"I have." Ellie took her seat beside Quinn and enjoyed the look of delight on Ruth's face. "It's like a time capsule in there."

"A very dusty, nasty one as well." Shirley shivered at the memory.

"I'm with you, Shirley," Quinn said. "Not a fan of closed spaces."

"Ruth and Shirley's dad built them a secret room through a closet in their bedroom," Ellie explained to the others. "I finally got around to visiting it."

"Thank you, dear," Ruth reached over and gave Ellie's hand a quick squeeze. "I'll cherish this even more now."

"So." Ellie looked at her group. "There are a few things to sort through." She pulled her ever-present notebook out, unclipped the pen, and clicked it open. "I've made a few notes about things we'll need to figure out. And Lennie, Tess and Doreen, I'm very sorry you won't be able to join us."

"I'm not one for sleeping in strange beds at the best of times," Lennie admitted.

"And the number of times I get up in the night." Doreen shook her head regretfully. "Well, I'm lucky my daughter has a grannie suite in her basement, so I'll get my own bathroom."

"But like I said," Tess jumped in, "we will expect a full report when you get back."

"Not to worry, Tess," Norma assured her.

"Right." Ellie looked at her list and over at the seniors. "How will we get everyone there?"

"Actually," Phil said, having been quiet until that point, "I've got a van that can hold us all quite comfortably. It's a 2000 Nissan Quest."

"Does it still run?" Shirley asked him.

"It does," he assured her. "Though I haven't driven it myself in a few years since they refused to renew my driver's license. But a friend of mine borrows it and keeps it in good shape."

"That's fantastic!" Ellie made a tick mark next to the transportation item on her list. "Aunt Norma, what are the sleeping arrangements in this cabin? Will there be enough beds? Will girls be split into one room and boys in another?"

"I'm pretty sure we're past that!" Norma pulled out a piece of paper from her pocket and pulled her glasses from the top of her head. "So, there's one bedroom with a double bed, which should go to Ruth and Jeremy. The second room has a double bed, with a single bed on top, like a bunk bed, and then another separate single bed. I thought Shirley, you, Phil and I could all have our own beds. I'll take the upper one."

"And what about Quinn and I?" Ellie asked, curious to see what her aunt had in store for them.

"Oh, there's a futon in the living room that turns into a lovely double bed." Norma looked over the top of her glasses at her niece. "Or is that making an assumption on my part?"

"Not there yet," Quinn answered with ease. "But we'll manage."

Ellie smiled at him, pleased with his response and his understanding that while their relationship was only months long, they hadn't taken that ultimate step yet. They had met in a most unconventional way, and they were still in the getting to know you phase. They weren't kids ruled by hormones, at least not totally, and they had a good idea of where the relationship was headed, just not sure when they'd get there.

"Phil." Norma got his attention. "Is that okay with you? Sharing a room with Shirley and I?"

"I *do* snore," he warned her.

"Don't we all!" Shirley laughed. "Among other noises."

"No, I have no problem with that," Phil said. "Though I will make at least one trip to the loo during the night, but I promise to be as quiet as I can."

"There may be a lineup!" Jeremy warned good-naturedly.

"So, are we all good with the sleeping arrangements?" Ellie asked, looking at each of them in turn. When they all nodded, she marked another item off her list.

"There wouldn't have been enough space for us even if we had been able to go," Lennie complained.

"Oh, no, Lennie," Norma said. "There is another cottage for you, Tess and Doreen, had you wanted to. I made sure of that."

"Maybe another time then," he muttered, more to himself.

"Oh, that sounds lovely." Tess gave him a bright smile.

"And what about food?" Ruth asked.

"Wait." Phil held up a hand. "How much will the cabin cost?"

"Nothing," Norma said. "I've already paid for it. I got a great senior's discount!"

"But..." he started.

"You're supplying the transportation, correct?" Norma asked him.

"Yes, but..."

"Then that's your part."

"And I'll pay the gas," Shirley said.

"I'm sure Maggie will make us some sandwiches and breakfast croissants from the Café, and Quinn and I are in charge of the supper meal, BBQ and salads," Ellie said. "We'll keep everything as easy as possible."

"Then Jeremy and I will supply the snacks and drinks," Ruth said.

"How does that sound to everyone?" Ellie asked after checking off the last item on her list.

"Sounds like this is going to be fun," Jeremy said. "I, for one, need a break from the rat race." They all laughed.

"This is very short notice," Ellie said. "Are you sure we all agree on everything?"

"It's one night and we don't need to pack a lot, do we?" Phil asked.

"So, how about Quinn and I pick up Phil around eight o'clock, and then we'll drop by and get everyone else along the way. Be ready for eight-thirty at the latest."

"Oh, I'm sure we'll all be on our porches long before that!" Shirley said.

"And," Ellie said loudly as they were all getting up and readying to leave. "There's a special place that we'll stop at on the way back. And it's a surprise, so don't even think about asking!"

Chapter Five

The rain pattered gently against the window as Ellie woke up and stretched. The minute she started moving, a furry head popped up at the side of her bed and licked her hand.

"Oh, go on with you," Ellie muttered, pushing the dog aside as she threw back the blankets and sat on the edge of the bed. "How did you get in here anyway?"

"My fault," Quinn said from the doorway. Even though the day was gloomy and the slobber remained on her fingers, seeing Quinn's smiling face was a great way to wake up. "Sorry about that."

"My gosh, you're already dressed!" Ellie said, jumping up in a panic. "Am I late? Did you let me sleep in?"

"Easy there." Quinn stepped inside and motioned for Cali to leave. He reached out and drew Ellie close for a good morning hug. "You've got plenty of time and everything is on schedule. Deep breath."

Ellie melted into the warmth of his arms and took that deep breath. "You smell like lemons."

Quinn released her and frowned. "It was the only soap in the shower. I'll have to get my own."

"No, no," Ellie protested. "I'm not complaining. You're paying rent to stay here, so you get to use the amenities. Should I buy you something else?"

He grinned. "I like lemon too. But I prefer the orange smell of your shampoo."

Ellie tilted her head and squinted at him. "Are you flirting with me?" She checked the clock on her bedside table. "At seven o'clock in the morning?"

"And if I was?"

"I have no response." She moved past him towards the bathroom, calling over her shoulder. "I won't be long and then we'll pack and take the furry beast to Maggie's."

"I'm packed, the dog's been walked, and her food is in the car."

Ellie turned slowly to stare at him. "Ruth is right. You *are* a keeper."

This time, it was Quinn who was at a loss for words.

***

By seven-thirty, they were ready to go. Cali jumped into the back of Ellie's car and within minutes they were knocking at the backdoor of the Cozy Corner Café.

When the door opened, glorious smells wafted out to greet them. The Café would open in half an hour, but the baking had been completed hours before and was now waiting to be placed on the trays.

"Come in, come in," Maggie said, standing back to let them pass. "It's a drizzly day out there. I hope that doesn't ruin your adventure."

Maggie and Ellie had been best friends since college, and had ended up living in Percyville at the same time through coincidence and being in the right place at the right time.

They headed straight into the business side of the café where Ellie paused and took a deep breath. "That sure smells good."

"Please don't tell me you didn't have breakfast," Maggie said, finishing the packing of all the sandwiches and goodies Ellie had ordered for the trip.

"No, she's fed," Quinn said. "Cleaned her plate so well, I thought she had licked it."

"For pity's sake!" Ellie said. "I have a good appetite."

"When someone else feeds you," Maggie said, winking at Quinn. "You guys are taking on quite a feat here, being cooped up with a bunch of old folk."

"Old folk?" Ellie said with a snort. "I bet some of those old folk could run circles around us all. And I wouldn't be organizing this if I didn't believe they were all more than capable of looking after themselves."

"They're really looking forward to finding buried treasure," Quinn said, putting Cali's food container on the floor by the counter. "Literally."

"You're more excited than they are," Ellie said, giving him a quick nudge with her elbow.

"Fair enough," Quinn nodded. "I guess I have a bit of the pirate in me, and I like the idea of finding buried treasure."

Ellie caught Maggie watching the interaction between Quinn and herself, and for once didn't feel uncomfortable. It was definitely time for her to live again, and Quinn seemed to know exactly what she needed. He reminded her of her late husband in that way, but everything else was purely original Quinn.

"So," Quinn said, moving things forward. "The beast has been walked. She's good for a bit and likely to curl up somewhere and watch the goings on."

Maggie came around the counter and handed the bags to Quinn before kneeling down beside Cali and giving her a deep head rub. Everyone knew that rubs were the way to Cali's heart. And a few treats. "I doubt we'll have any problems with this lovely lady. Customers will adore her."

"But you can't keep her near the food, right?" Ellie asked worriedly. "We don't want you to get into trouble or anything."

"She'll be stationed in the back room and it's only for a couple of days," Maggie said. "And I'll take her for long walks in your forest, too."

The front door slammed open and a wind-blown Daphne ran in, forcing the door closed behind her. "Sorry about that. The wind just grabbed it out of my hands." She caught sight of Cali and within minutes, she was on the ground, loving Cali up. "This is going to be a great day. We have a dog!"

"She's only borrowed," Ellie said, laughing at the joy on Daphne's face. "Enjoy her while you can."

"And now we're off," Quinn said. "Wish us luck."

"I can't wait to hear the stories when you get back!" Maggie said.

Quinn opened the door with one hand and held the bags with the other, while Ellie dashed out into the rain to open the car doors. It would be impossible not to get damp on a morning such as this.

***

Phil was sliding his suitcase into the back of a dark blue van when Ellie and Quinn arrived ten minutes later. The rain had eased, but they were all dressed for the coolness of the hour.

Quinn parked the car beside the van, where he'd leave it for the next couple of days. Ellie hopped out and greeted Phil with a hug.

"Oh, my," Phil said in surprise, giving her a gentle hug in return. "Good morning to you two. You both look like you're heading out for an exciting trip."

"You know me, Phil." Ellie stepped back and grinned. "I do so love a family adventure!"

"Good morning, Phil." Quinn took his and Ellie's bags, plus the bags of packed food from the car and put them in the back of the van. "I see you're ready to go."

"I am. But do you think there's enough room for everyone to be comfortable?" Worriedly Phil stretched to look in the windows and count the number of seats to himself. "It's a long ride for us."

Quinn gazed inside and nodded. "I don't see a problem. Very nice vehicle, by the way."

Phil's expression cleared. He straightened his back with pride and nodded. "It was one of my indulgences. Having a lot of grandchildren, even though they live all over, it was good to have excess seating. And I love the ride. Let me lock up and we can go get everyone else."

Once all settled in the van, Quinn headed to the Tiny House Haven for Ruth, Shirley and Jeremy. Jeremy had stayed the night with the ladies, believing it would take less time to collect everyone that way.

As they pulled up to the house, they noticed the bustle of figures behind the front door before it was flung open. Jeremy strode onto the porch, suitcase in hand, a smile on his face. He gave them a quick wave and then disappeared back inside to return with two more suitcases.

Quinn jumped out and gathered the bags, depositing them into the back of the van. He stepped up to the porch and offered Ruth a hand down the stairs, as Jeremy still needed the support of the handrail. His knee surgery had been a success, and he was heeding the doctor's advice to take his rehab gently and seriously. Stairs could be tricky, but he didn't shy away from them.

Shirley locked the front door and joined them at the van as they selected the seats they wanted. "I don't mind sitting in the back," Shirley said, waiting for Quinn to push one chair forward before she climbed in with the barest amount of struggle. "Oh, this is so nice," she said as she settled into the seat, strapping the seatbelt closed around her. "I thought you said it was a 2000, Phil."

Phil turned towards her. "It is, but I only used it when the grandkids were around, or I needed to pick up something big. It's been gently used."

Quinn helped Ruth and Jeremy into the seats beside Phil, closed the door and dashed around to jump into the driver's seat just as the rain started pounding against the roof.

"Well," Shirley raised her voice above the noise, "I hope this doesn't last all day. My joints won't take too kindly to it."

Ellie looked back at her. "I have it on good authority from the weather lady that the rain will be spotty from here on out, and there's no rain forecasted at all for the Lake Samson area."

"You know how I feel about weather people," Shirley muttered.

"They'd have you wearing layers of clothes during a heatwave!" Jeremy laughed.

It took another few minutes to reach Norma's house, and by then the rain had eased enough that Norma didn't have to sprint to the van to stay dry. Quinn tucked her small bag in with the others and helped her squeeze in behind Ruth to sit beside Shirley in the back.

"Well, this is nice," Norma pronounced with satisfaction. "Good morning, one and all."

As the van pulled away, the rain picked up once again. And the windshield wipers started to squeak.

"Can you fix that noise, Quinn?" Shirley called from the back. "That is more than a little annoying. We don't have to listen to that for the entire drive, do we?"

"It's an old van, Shirley," Phil said. "Sorry about that."

"The wipers must be dry," Quinn said.

The squeak sounded again, loud and center stage. Now everyone was focused on the noise.

"Oh, for goodness sake," Norma said. "Stop and let me out. Quinn, I'll need your help." Norma rummaged in her bag and removed a bottle.

"It's raining, Norma," Quinn said as he pulled off the road.

"Are you made of sugar?" she asked.

Ellie grinned at Quinn as he hopped out and helped Norma from her seat. They weren't getting soaking wet, but the rain was dampening their shoulders.

"Here." Phil passed them an umbrella and Quinn opened it, holding it over Norma's head as the little woman walked toward the front of the van.

Those inside couldn't hear the conversation, but they watched as Norma held up her bottle, dragged a tissue from her pocket and motioned for Quinn to rub it up and down the windshield wipers. She saturated the tissue with the liquid and gave it to him.

Taking the umbrella from Quinn, she held it up as he leaned in and wiped the left wiper thoroughly. He held the tissue out to her, and she sprayed it again. This time they moved to the other side of the van where Quinn repeated the process on the right wiper.

With umbrella still in hand, Norma returned to the door, handed it to Quinn, then climbed back up into her seat. Quinn hurried to the driver's seat, and they were off.

Everyone held their breath as the wipers swiped back and forth.

And not a squeak was heard.

"Well, I'll be!" Shirley said. "What did you do?"

"Rubbing alcohol," Norma said, jamming the bottle back into her bag. "WD-40 is better, but it's all I had."

The next few minutes were filled with small talk, unreliable weather reports, and how comfortable the transportation had turned out to be. The rain intensified for a few miles, spattering the windows and creating a cocoon inside the van. Half an hour later, the sky had cleared, the sun was shining, and Shirley was wondering if they would need air conditioning before too long.

They left civilization shortly after, driving off the highway and onto a long dirt road that would almost lead to the front door of Virginia's Cabins. And that's when the engine sputtered once, twice, then died.

Quinn pulled over to the side of the road and everyone sat still.

"I thought the van was in great shape," Shirley said, shifting nervously.

"It is," Phil defended, his face flushing in embarrassment.

"Let me look." Quinn got out and opened the hood. Norma followed, standing beside him, with Ellie right behind them. The women watched as Quinn fiddled with one thing, then another. "I can't see..."

"Have you got a flashlight?" Norma asked. She pulled herself up on the front bumper.

"Aunt Norma!" Ellie said, reaching to steady her aunt. "What the heck are you doing?"

"Just get me that flashlight, please." Norma raised an eyebrow at Quinn. Wordlessly he headed to the back of the van.

"You don't know anything about cars and engines," Ellie said.

Before Norma could respond, Quinn was putting a small flashlight into her hand. "Phil didn't have one in the kit, but Ruth had one. I'll never be surprised again by what women carry in their purses."

"We'll be the saviour of civilization," Norma muttered as she shone the light inside. "Ah, that's what I thought."

Quinn bobbed his head back and forth, trying to see what she was doing, but his view was blocked. He caught Ellie's surprised look and shrugged.

Norma snaked her small arm into the engine and grasped a hose, wiggled it around and twisted it tight. "Dang it!" She straightened and stretched her back.

"Let me try," Quinn said, about to move into place.

"Cool your jets," Norma said. "I've got this." She leaned down again and continued her struggle. "That should do it," she said. "But I'll need a wrench."

Quinn hurried back to the trunk and returned with the requested tool.

Norma thanked him for it, then carefully tightened the clamp, gave it another wiggle and handed the wrench back to Quinn. She eased down off the bumper and returned to her seat as if nothing unusual had happened.

Quinn and Ellie looked at each other, the seniors hidden from view by the open hood. "What was that?" Quinn whispered to her.

Ellie shrugged. "I don't know how she did that."

Quinn dropped the hood and after replacing the tool, they returned to their seats. When the van started without a problem, everyone gave Quinn a cheer. "Well done, Quinn," Shirley called from the back.

"It wasn't me," he said, driving off slowly, as if expecting something else to go wrong.

"It was Norma." Ellie turned to see Norma shrug.

"Something I picked up." Norma stared out the window at the passing scenery, obviously not wanting to carry on the conversation.

"So," Ellie looked at her group, "has anyone got an interesting or favorite vacation to share?"

"Well." Jeremy drew out the word, as if searching for the memory. "I do."

"Let's get settled then," Ruth said, turning slightly so she didn't have to crane her neck around to see him.

"It was the first trip my son, Sam and I went on together." Jeremy paused, lost in thought.

"Where did you go?" Phil asked.

"Oh, we went camping, to Voyageur Provincial Park, near Hawkesbury in Ontario. Lovely camp. We had a two-man tent, which was too small, but thankfully Sam was only six years old and didn't take up too much space!"

"I would have taken you for a tent trailer kind of guy," Shirley said from behind him. "Something a bit more comfortable than sleeping on the ground."

"Believe me," Jeremy laughed, "had I been able to afford it, I would have. We brought under-padding for our sleeping bags, but my body did not enjoy it. Sam did though."

"And what made this vacation memorable?" Ellie asked.

"Well, besides it being our first camping trip, it was when Sam almost drowned."

"Oh, heavens!" Ruth sputtered. "How awful!"

Jeremy took her hand in his and held it tight. "It turned out okay, Ruthie. He was fine. I, on the other hand, learned a precious lesson. You can look away for a split second and disaster can strike." He snapped his fingers sharply to emphasize his point.

"But you obviously saved him." Phil frowned at the thought of Jeremy almost losing his son.

"I did," Jeremy nodded. "I ran into the water so fast that I left waves behind me. I grabbed him up and out, and he was already coughing as I put him over my shoulder. I threw him on the ground, and was about to start CPR when he coughed up some water and sat up. A crowd had gathered, and a woman brought a towel and wrapped Sam up in it. But I remember feeling the sun burning my back, the heat on my head, the cries of the birds on the beach. It was all so ... brilliant, the light, the sound. It was overwhelming, actually. And then Sam said

"Dad, can we get an ice cream?" Jeremy let out a deep breath and sat back in his seat, unaware that he had hunched forward in telling the tale.

Quiet filled the van as they all pictured the scene he had described. Ruth leaned into him. "And you can never keep a child away from their ice cream, even when they almost drown."

Norma let out a small laugh from the back, but tried to stifle it. "Sorry."

"No need, Norma," Jeremy said, shaking his head. "Ruth is right. A child's mind is solely on themselves at that age. As I said, lesson learned on my part. I became a bit of a hawk after that, watching too closely. Until I realized Sam was a level-headed boy, and for the most part he knew how not to get into trouble."

"Do you mean he bamboozled you?" Norma asked.

"More like I had to remember what I was like at his age," Jeremy answered. "That's when I started to really see a lot more of what was happening in his life. But we did go camping again. We visited as many provincial campgrounds as we could, invested in a bigger tent, and we even returned to Voyageur, because that's where our love of camping began."

"Hmm," Phil said.

"Phil," Ellie turned to him, "do you have something to share?"

Phil frowned, then he squared his shoulders. "Not to do with camping. But I need to remind you again I snore. All this talk about sleeping in tight quarters and all. I may have mentioned it before, but it's been brought to my attention that ... it's quite noisy. So, I'm apologizing and offering to sleep out on the futon on my own."

"Phil," Shirley said from the back, "you're a peach! It's only for one night, and I doubt any of us will sleep well. But I do promise to poke you if it gets too loud. Us old folk deserve comfortable beds and the futon is for the kids."

"Did she just call us kids?" Quinn asked Ellie.

"She did. Isn't that wonderful?"

"I was wondering," Jeremy asked, "Is there any place along here with a comfort station?"

"There is," Norma said. "There's a small gas station around the next..."

Before she could complete her comment, they turned a corner in the road and up ahead was a big sign declaring *Gas and Eats Available Here*.

"Oh, thank goodness!" he muttered.

Quinn pulled into the convenience store and opened the doors to let everyone out. There were no other cars in the parking lot. The building was small and well maintained. The pumps glistened as if they had been polished an hour before. The smell was not of gas, but of fir trees. A squirrel dashed across the pavement as Jeremy headed in to get the key to the washroom.

"Might as well all take a break," Shirley said, clambering out after Norma and stretching in the sun. "How much longer until we get there?"

"I'd say only about half an hour or so," Norma said.

Phil and Shirley used the facilities, and Quinn topped off the gas tank. Shirley went into the store and paid for the gas and then everyone piled back into the van. Moments later, they were on the road and the first sign announcing *Virginia's Cabins 20 Miles* greeted them around the next bend.

"When was the last time we used miles in Canada?" Phil asked.

"A long time ago," Norma muttered.

"So, it hasn't been updated in decades," Shirley shook her head at the weathered sign as they passed.

"That sign is older than Ellie is!" Quinn laughed.

"But she looks a lot better," Ruth chided him.

"Nothing flaky about her," Quinn watched Ellie turn to her window to hide her grin.

"I hope the cabins are not as old," Shirley said.

Chapter Six

The *Welcome to Virginia's Cabins* sign loomed ahead, its paint flaking, the once vibrant colors of the water and trees faded now to a pale glimmer of what they had once been. Quinn drove down the treelined road to the main building and parked in the empty customer space.

The group eased from the van and looked around. Even though Norma had told them they were the only clients there until noon the next day, it was quiet. Even the birds weren't singing.

"Thankfully, it's sunny," Shirley said.

"I bet they could film a horror movie here," Phil said, looking around as if expecting a crazy killer to dash out of the forest.

"I remember the sign out front, actually," Quinn said, "My brother, Owen, made a film near here and we passed the Virginia's Cabins sign quite a few times."

"This spot is not only off the beaten path, but there are no developments nearby," Norma told them. "It's usually quiet all the time, except when packed with people. You'll be surprised how quickly the animals show themselves, though, especially if you have food on you. I'll check us in at the office, then we'll drive down to our cabin."

An overhead bell tinkled when they entered, Quinn and Ellie following Norma to the reception area. The desk was unmanned, but the sound of thumping feet came to them from down the staircase from the second floor.

"Hello, hello," said the deep voice of a large man who stepped behind the counter. His hair was wet and his shirt buttoned incorrectly. He looked like he had jumped from the shower minutes before and grabbed whatever clothes he could find.

"Oh, welcome," said a tiny woman who followed him. She was the man's opposite, much more elegant for a cabin rental operation than one would expect. Smartly pressed white blouse and tailored black pants, her hair in a bun. The couple couldn't be older than forty.

"Are you Anna Wagner?" Norma asked. "I believe we spoke on the phone last night."

"Yes, yes," the man said, his German accent heavy but understandable. "You spoke with my wife. I am Otto Wagner, owner of the Virginia's Cabins." He said the last with pride, nodding at them in greeting.

Anna raised an eyebrow at Norma, who responded in kind. "Nice to meet you both," Norma said.

Ellie took a minute to look around the office. A bulletin board on one wall held a single pamphlet from the local fire department warning about the proper use of campfires. Another wall held shelves of candy bars and chips, while a cooler in the corner contained soft drinks and ice. The whole place looked run down and tired.

"You are renting the big cabin for one night, correct?" Mr. Wagner threw open his ledger and trailed a finger down the page to an entry halfway along. "Norma?" He looked at her.

"That's me," Norma said. "I must thank you for waiving your normal two-night requirement for a stay."

"Geld ist geld," he said under his breath.

"Yes, indeed," Norma smiled at him. "Money is money."

Ellie glanced at Quinn and saw the same realization in his eyes–Norma understood German?

The couple also seemed surprised, but Mr. Wagner filled in the ledger in record time and turned it around for Norma to sign. She pulled out her wallet and passed her card across the Interac machine that Anna put on the counter. Collecting her bill, she held out her hand for the key.

"What time is check out tomorrow?" Norma asked.

"Oh, we like people gone by eleven," Mr. Wagner said, closing his ledger and taking a step back.

"But we can give you a little extra time," his wife said, smiling as if to compensate for her husband's rudeness. "Perhaps noon would be good?"

Mr. Wagner gave his wife a quizzical look but nodded at them, as if the idea had been his to begin with. "Yes, yes, that will be fine," he said.

"I'm curious," Norma said to Anna. "I came here when I was a child, for many years. When did you buy the business?"

"Oh, it's been about five years now," Anna said. "The family who owned it had other people managing it for many years. And then they decided to sell it."

"And we were in the right place at the right time," boomed Mr. Wagner, once again puffing himself up as if he had bought the cabins in an amazing turn of events.

Quinn put his hand out to him. "Good to meet you, Mr. Wagner. You have a lovely place here." He took Mr. Wagner's hand and gave it a firm shake before following Ellie and Norma out.

"What was that all about?" Ellie asked. "The macho handshake thing."

"I have no idea what you're talking about," Quinn said as he slipped behind the wheel. "Sometimes it's a good way to take the measure of a person."

"A handshake?" Ellie did not believe him.

"He's right, Ellie," Norma said before getting back into the van beside Shirley. "You'd be shocked what a handshake can reveal about a person."

"And since when do you understand German?" Ellie asked, getting everyone's attention with the question.

Phil peered around Ruth to see Norma. "Seriously? You speak German?"

"I was always good at languages," Norma said, and hastily changed the topic. "Quinn, if you follow this road to the left, the cabin we're staying at is the last one at the very end."

"Would you look at this," Ruth said as they drove slowly past other small cabins, each spaced a decent distance from the other. "It's like a little wonderland in here."

"Oh, my," Ellie said as Quinn parked at the end of the road beside a large cabin. "This is impressive."

They all eased out of the van and made their way to the foot of the stairs. The birds had started chattering above, and the wind was swishing through the branches, bringing a warm smell of fir trees.

Quinn went to the back of the van and handed out everyone's suitcases, before taking his and Ellie's, and the packed food bags before locking the vehicle.

"It's lovely," Ruth whispered, gazing up at the quaint-looking cabin.

"Why are you whispering?" Shirley asked as she made her way to the front and headed up the stairs. "Who's got the key?"

Norma met her at the door and unlocked it, holding it open as they all passed her. Except for Quinn, who took the door and ushered her inside. "Thank you, kind sir." She winked at him.

Ruth stood just inside, her bag on the floor. "This is perfect."

Norma stepped forward and motioned with her hand. "Obviously this is the living room, and you can see the dining table."

"The table is huge!" Phil said.

"Exactly what we need for puzzles," Ruth said.

"The kitchen is behind it," Norma continued. "And to the left is the smaller bedroom, for Ruth and Jeremy, the bathroom in between, and at the far end is the bigger bedroom."

"It's very cozy." Shirley nodded her head as if her approval was the final stamp needed for a pleasant stay.

"And no TV or computer in sight!" Phil said. "Trust me, that's a good thing right now. I didn't realize how much I needed to get away for a while." He walked to the open front window and took a deep breath. "You can smell the lake! This is my idea of heaven."

"Considering we all live in the country," Shirley said, giving him a gentle smile, "this can't be too different."

"No, you're right," Phil said. "But it's not home, so it's definitely special."

They fanned out, going from room to room, checking out the space and claiming their beds by dropping their bags on them.

Ellie walked into the largest bedroom and looked around. The bunk was a double on the bottom, single on the top with an easy to climb ladder. A separate single bed was up against a wall that let the sleeper gaze out the window. "Is everyone happy with this arrangement?"

"Don't say I didn't warn you about the snoring," Phil said from the single bed.

"And I'm tickled to be sleeping in an upper bunk!" Norma said as she climbed the ladder nimbly and tossed her bag onto the bed. "Just like when I was a kid."

"This will do nicely," Shirley said, sitting on the lower bunk and testing the comfort of the mattress.

"Our room is lovely too," Ruth said from behind them. "It even has a little washbasin!"

"And it looks out over the lake," Jeremy added.

"But what about you, dear?" Norma asked Ellie. "Will you and Quinn manage on the futon?"

Ellie hadn't checked it out, but wandered out to the living room to find Quinn eyeing their sleeping spot. The others followed.

"I think it'll be fine," Quinn said, though he didn't sound totally convinced that his six-foot two body would fit on the futon.

"Oh, I'm sure it will be," Shirley smirked.

"And we're all pretty deaf," Jeremy said, "so we won't hear anything."

"You shouldn't tease them," Ruth said.

"Well, it's not like we haven't all been ... peppy in our lives at one time." Phil stole a glance at Shirley.

"Speak for yourself, peppy man," Shirley said, her grin easing the words as she headed back to her room.

"You'll manage," Norma nudged Ellie and winked, noticing how red her niece had gotten.

"Wait a second," Shirley called out. "Where are the sheets?"

Ellie and Norma hurried back to find Shirley pulling up the comforters on all the beds. Not one of them had linens, only mattresses with mattress covers.

"What the heck?" Norma hurried into Ruth and Jeremy's room only to return, shaking her head. "Same there too. This is not acceptable."

"Not to worry," Ellie said in her best soothing voice. "Let's find the linen closet and I'll make them up in no time."

Like a group of ducks, each turning this way and that, their heads swivelling, they concluded that there was no linen closet in the entire cabin.

"What about towels?" Phil asked, stepping into the bathroom. "Nothing!"

"We're paying good money for this place," Shirley said. "Or at least Norma is. This is intolerable."

Norma headed for the front door, Ellie on her heels.

"Where are you going?" Quinn asked.

"I'm going to have a word with Mr. and Mrs. Wagner," Norma muttered under her breath. Her jaw was clenched and everyone would swear later that they saw steam coming out of her ears.

"Right behind you," Quinn said, nodding at Ellie to follow.

Chapter Seven

Norma swung her arms, clenched her fists, and tightened her shoulders as she stomped down the porch steps and headed along the path. She was on a mission.

Ellie took hold of her aunt's arm to slow her down. "Whoa there, Aunt Norma, let us catch up!"

"You look like you're about to storm a beach in France," Quinn said. "I know this is upsetting, but take a breath before you start yelling."

His comment froze Norma in her tracks. She turned to Quinn, a frown on her face. "I wasn't going to yell."

Ellie tilted her head to the side and squinted at her. "That's not what it looks like." She'd known her aunt all her life, and while yelling was not her normal response, she definitely spoke her mind.

Norma released a deep breath and started walking again. "I'm sorry. I wanted this trip to be something special, for everyone to enjoy this place as much as I have. But now there are all kinds of things happening and—"

"Not all kinds," Ellie said, giving her aunt's arm a gentle squeeze. "Just this one. And once we get the linens, we'll set things to right."

"We'll have the beds made in no time and then you can show us around," Quinn said, opening the office door, waiting for the ladies to go inside.

The door slipped through Quinn's fingers and slammed behind them as they stood by the reception desk and waited. When no footsteps came thumping down the stairs, Norma hit the bell a few times.

Movement from the back alerted them to Otto's arrival. He came through, wiping his hands on a towel. "Yes?" His manners had not improved.

"We have no bedsheets or towels," Norma said. She held his gaze, as if daring him to contradict her. But all he did was stare down at the towel.

"What did you say?" Anna appeared from behind her husband, her voice low and confused.

"We have no bedsheets and towels," Norma repeated. "Nothing at all."

Anna turned to her husband and gave him the evil eye. "Is this true? I ask you one thing, Otto, one thing, while we are so busy. Take the clean sheets and make the beds. Leave a towel on each bed. We have *one* cabin to look after today, just one! Was that too hard for you to do?"

Otto looked at his wife and her furious expression and took a step back. "I'm sorry, I forgot."

Anna pushed past him and headed to the back room. "You forgot, you forgot. If I didn't do everything around here, we wouldn't have a business."

Norma, Ellie and Quinn exchanged worried looks with Otto, and he gave them a weak smile. "She's going to get them. I'm very sorry." The apology sounded as if he'd dragged it from the soles of his feet.

Anna came bustling back, struggling to hold a basket full of bedsheets and towels. "I'll take care of this. I'm so sorry," she told them as she headed out the door. "You can't get good help these days."

"May I?" Quinn held his hands out for the basket, and after a second of hesitation, she gave him a nod and handed it to him. And then she marched ahead, mumbling under her breath about how useless certain people were.

They followed her back to their cabin, not wanting to intrude on her obvious task. Anna opened the door and waited until she had everyone's attention.

"I must apologize for this inconvenience," she said, looking each senior in the eye.

"Well, it's not bed time yet, so there's no harm done," Phil said, tacking on a smile, which Anna didn't return.

“I will have everything completed in a few minutes.” Anna motioned for Quinn to follow her into the first bedroom.

“We’ll help,” Ellie assured her. She took a set of sheets into the larger bedroom and made Phil’s bed.

“And we’ll share out the towels,” Ruth said, taking them from the basket and handing one to each of them. “I guess we can keep them on our beds for now.”

Anna and Quinn finished Ruth and Jeremy’s bed in minutes, before Anna moved into the big room to make up Shirley’s bed.

“I’ll take those,” Ellie said, grabbing another set of sheets and making quick work of Norma’s upper bunk bed. Within fifteen minutes, all the beds were made to Anna’s satisfaction.

“I’ll leave these here.” Anna put a final set on the end table near the futon. She looked around and checked that everything else was to her liking before turning to the group one last time. “So, if you need anything, anything at all, you come to see me. I will make this right.”

“Don’t worry, Anna,” Norma said. “It was a little mix-up, but it’s all sorted out.”

Anna gave Norma a wobbly smile and nodded. “That’s very kind of you. Running a business like this is difficult with only the two of us. And we have a full house starting tomorrow, and there’s still so much to do. But all my husband can think about is painting that stupid apartment above the office.”

Ruth reached out and patted her shoulder. “You’ll be fine, dear. You’re obviously an organized person. That’s half the battle. Don’t worry about us. You won’t even know we’re here.”

“Well, at least it will be a quiet night,” Anna said. “Some nights we have to go to cabins at all hours, reminding guests others are trying to sleep.”

“No, you won’t have that kind of trouble with us,” Jeremy laughed. “And no singing either!”

“So, I will leave you to enjoy your stay.” Anna closed the door quietly and took off down the path to the office.

"She seems like a nice young lady," Shirley said.

"I may have been mistaken as to who wears the pants in that family," Norma said. "Now come on, let me show you around."

Norma headed out the front door and waited for the others to join her at the foot of the steps. She pointed the way they had come. "Between the office and here, there are six other cabins and a few spots for people with tents. They're quite lovely, actually."

"Let's go for a little walk and see them," Ruth suggested.

"It'll take us till lunchtime to get there and back," Phil warned.

"So be it," Shirley said as she headed down the path. "We'll be famished when we're done."

"Norma, I hope you don't mind, but I'm going to talk to Quinn about ... fishing, at the dock," Jeremy said. The last words came out in a rush, as if having popped into his head that very moment. He looked at Quinn and jerked his head towards the dock. "Phil, do you want to join us?"

"Thanks, but I'm not a fan of water," Phil said, with no embarrassment. "Can't swim, so I keep my distance. It's worked all my life. I'll chaperone the ladies, if you don't mind."

"And I could use a bit of steadying on this path," Shirley said, putting her arm through Phil's, to the shock of everyone. "Come on, all, adventure is afoot!"

"Right." Quinn picked up on the subtle head movement from Jeremy and followed him towards the water.

Ellie watched them go, both men ending up on the dock, hands moving as if in animated conversation. Then suddenly they both turned to look her way.

She waved.

They waved.

Ellie narrowed her eyes. Something was up but she'd let it be for now. She caught up with the group at the first cabin past theirs, and listened as Norma told funny stories of the families who had stayed there long ago.

Chapter Eight

"Do you fish, Jeremy?" Quinn asked. He noticed that the older man had not once looked at the lake.

"Never in my life!"

"So, what's going on?"

Jeremy shuffled, stole a quick glance at the group disappearing around a cabin in the distance, and let out a deep breath. "I need your help."

"Sure, anything." Quinn liked this gentleman, and he truly was a gentle man. Quinn especially approved of how he treated Ruth. Having found each other after decades apart, and then reconnecting, had given them both renewed lives.

"I'm going to ask Ruth to marry me," Jeremy whispered, as if afraid his voice would carry across the water. He plunged his hands into the pockets of his jacket, then pulled them out just as fast, unsure what to do next.

"Congratulations!" Quinn gave him a quick handshake, realizing that if anyone saw them, they'd figure out the guys were not talking about fishing. "When are you going to ask her, and how?"

Jeremy looked around nervously, unable to stay still, but taking some weight off his recently repaired knee. "Well, it has to be romantic. This is a lovely place, and I want her to remember it forever, or as long as we have left!"

Quinn let his eyes skim the setting they were in. The calm water, the trees hugging the shoreline, the sound of birds, and the rustling in the bushes of tiny animals all together created a peaceful atmosphere. "It *is* lovely. And Ruth deserves something special. How about..." His gaze zeroed in on the canoes at the far end of the beach, stacked neatly by the office. "What about a boat ride?"

Jeremy looked at the boats Quinn motioned to and smiled. "I haven't been in a canoe for ages, but that would be perfect. I'll ask her to go for a paddle after lunch."

"I'll be right back." Quinn jogged down the beach and into the office. Minutes later, he had a red canoe hefted over his head and was making his way down the sand. He dropped the boat on the dock and held up a finger before heading back.

Jeremy saw Anna standing on her porch with something in her hands. Quinn took them from her and rejoined Jeremy with a paddle and two lifejackets. Anna waved at him from the office and he returned the gesture. She was obviously trying her best to make their stay memorable.

"Gosh," Jeremy said under his breath, "what am I doing?"

"Something you've wanted to do since you were a teenager," Quinn grinned. "I have to tell you, Jeremy, and if you repeat this, we will have words. I think this whole romance thing is exciting as heck."

"You shouldn't be worried about people knowing you're a softie, Quinn," Jeremy said. "Everyone knows already!"

The sound of voices reached them as the group made their way back to the cabin.

"Did you catch any fish?" Ellie asked, noting the canoe on the dock, but choosing to ignore it for now.

"I don't think we'll have enough time for that, unfortunately," Jeremy said. He took Ruth's hand and guided her to a couple of chairs near the fire pit. "Oof, it's good to sit down!"

The others took seats as well, each sinking back and relaxing, sheltered from the sun by an enormous tree.

"I'm going to get lunch and we'll eat out here," Ellie said. "Is that okay with everyone?"

"Indeed, it is." Phil rubbed his stomach. "That gurgling sound you hear is my daily reminder it's noon."

Ruth started to rise, but Ellie held up a hand. "No, you don't, Ruth. Quinn and I have this. Sit back and relax for a bit. "

When Ellie had Quinn alone in the cabin, she whirled on him and whispered, "What the heck is going on?"

Quinn froze, his eyes darting anywhere but at Ellie. "I have no idea what you mean."

"Oh, for pity's sake," Ellie opened the fridge and took out the sandwiches they had transferred from their cooler bags and put them on a tray. Without looking away from him, she grabbed the bags of chips on the counter and tossed them to him. "I wasn't born yesterday, you know. What does Jeremy have up his sleeve?"

"Well," Quinn said, lowering his voice as he got close to Ellie and whispered in her ear. "He's going to ask Ruth to marry him."

"What?!" Ellie slapped her hand across her mouth so she wouldn't make another peep. "What?" She asked again, this time in a furious whisper, her cheeks wide with a grin.

"Don't say a word. It's a surprise," Quinn hushed.

"Not a word." Ellie crossed her heart with her finger. "Oh, this is so amazing. It's even better than finding Norma's buried treasure!"

Quinn knew how much Ruth meant to Ellie, how the woman had helped her when Ellie's husband and daughter had died a few years before, and how much it meant to have Ruth in her life. "Yeah, it is pretty cool."

"How will I ever stay quiet?" Ellie muttered to herself as she gathered napkins and put everything on the tray.

"Because you can't wait to see the reaction when he asks her, right?" He waited for her nod, but worried about the twinkle in her eye and the huge grin. "Come here." He pulled her close and kissed her deeply. "There, now you look like you have something to smile about."

Ellie watched him head out the door with the tray, now piled high with chip bags and sandwiches. She followed behind with the box of drinks, grin still firmly in place.

***

When they'd finished lunch, and the sandwich wrappings were cleared away, Ellie brought out her laptop and placed it on the picnic table.

"So, like I said before, I think it'll be interesting to add some facts about our ancestors who came before us. Is there anyone you want to know more about?" She booted up the computer and was relieved to find the Wi-Fi signal quite strong.

"Here," Norma passed her a piece of paper. "I took down the password from the office."

"When did you do that?" Ellie asked. She knew for a fact that Norma had not been in the office alone, and couldn't remember seeing her do it.

"I wrote it down when we got back. It was on the wall." Norma shrugged. "You didn't see it?"

"There was a lot going on with the Wagners, so no, I wasn't paying attention."

"You should," Norma said. "It could save your life one day."

"I'd like to find someone," Quinn said. Everyone looked surprised, as Quinn had never participated in any of the meetings before. "My grandfather, the one who lived in Montreal and met my grandmother here when she was visiting. They were married within months. It was quite the whirlwind romance, and the family back in Scotland were not happy about her staying here. I'd only met him twice before he died."

"And what was your grandfather's name?" Ellie asked.

"Fergus Anderson," Quinn said.

"And when did he die?" Ellie asked. "I want to set my search parameters within a certain time frame, so we don't get anyone who might not be your grandfather. Saves time."

"Right." Quinn hesitated, trying to remember the date. "I think he died in the nineties."

"Good enough," Ellie said.

"And what site are you using?" Ruth asked, taking Jeremy's hand it hers, entwining their fingers comfortably. Hand holding had become their favorite mode of connection.

"I'm going to use Newspapers.com to start. I'll do a global search," Ellie said as she typed. "The great thing about this site is you *can* do a global search. But if you want to narrow it, you can go by country, by city, by newspaper and then by date. For now, I've put in his name, a broad time range from, let's say 1920 to 1970, and we'll enter Quebec, Canada to start." She hit the magnifying glass icon and waited. She sat forward with a jolt and looked at Quinn, eyebrows raised.

"What did you find?" he asked, leaving his seat to hunker down beside her to study the screen. "There are a lot of entries."

"Not really," Ellie said. "And they might not all be related to him. There are only six, so let's check them out by date."

"For goodness sake, Quinn," Jeremy said, "get a chair. Watching you crouch like that is making my new knee hurt!"

Quinn grabbed his chair and settled in beside Ellie. "Right, what's first?" He squinted at the screen, and Ellie gave him a curious look.

"Do you need glasses?"

"I have them," he answered, "but I don't enjoy wearing them."

"So, you'd prefer not to see things clearly?" Ruth asked in surprise.

"No," he drawled. "I just wear them when I'm not with..." He stopped talking as he realized how that sounded. "It's not an ego thing. I got teased a lot when I was younger. It's a hard habit to let go of."

"Wait." Ellie held up a hand as if to say stop right there. "I have *never* seen you wearing glasses!"

"You've walked in on me while I'm working," he said.

"But those are work glasses," she sputtered. "To keep the dust and stuff from getting in your eyes. Safety goggles."

"Prescription safety goggle." He grinned at her.

"Quinn," Ruth said in her teacher voice, "go get your glasses please. That squinty face is not appealing."

Without another word, he went to his bag and rummaged for his glasses case before he returned to Ellie's side. He held his glasses up to the sun, pulled his shirt out of his jeans, and cleaned them off before putting them on. Not once did he look at the surrounding faces.

"Well," Norma said from across the fire pit. "You look very handsome."

"You mean more handsome than usual?" Shirley asked, joining in the teasing.

"Oh, certainly, he can't be more handsome!" Ruth laughed.

"Okay," Quinn said. His face turned red, but he refused to give in to their teasing. "I get it."

"Fine," Ellie said with a snort, "we all agree he's handsome. Can we get back to the good stuff?"

"I bet he is the good stuff," Norma whispered a little too loudly to Shirley.

"You women are terrible." Phil shook his head.

"So," Ellie said a little louder, "I have the Montreal Star here on June 12, 1947, that's the first, so let's open that—oh, my."

"What? What?" Jeremy asked.

Quinn read the article from the screen and shook his head. "No, that can't be my grandfather. He would never..."

Ellie placed a hand on his and gave it a squeeze. "Let me read the entire article for everyone, and then we'll see what it means." Ellie took a deep breath and started to read.

"On Thursday, the 8th of May, Mr. Fergus Anderson, of 57 13Th Avenue in Rosemount was arrested for the murder of Carl Watkins, of 23 Ridge Avenue. Mr. Watkins had been stabbed repeatedly in an alley five streets from his home and discovered in the early hours by a paperboy. The investigation is ongoing."

"Wait," Quinn said, a frown creasing his forehead. "How do they know my grandfather killed this guy? What's the evidence? What's the motive? Were there witnesses?"

"Hang on," Ellie said, returning her attention to the computer. "There's another article from two days later."

"Following further investigation Mr. Watkins had been seen in a state of drunkenness on the evening of May 6th, when he came out of the Green Ghost on St. Urbain St. He fell into the wife of Mr. Anderson, who was passing by with her husband at the time, causing her to fall to the ground. She was rushed to the hospital where she subsequently lost the child she was carrying. Witnesses report how distraught Mr. Anderson was at the time and how he carried his wife to a nearby taxi."

"Oh, my goodness!" Ruth said, a hand to her mouth.

"Wait, there's more," Ellie said.

"With motive in place, officers went to the residence of Mr. Anderson and arrested him for the murder of Mr. Watkins two nights later. Mr. Anderson will appear in court before a Judge in three days time to enter a plea. He protested his innocence when being put into a patrol van and shouted to his wife that this was all a mistake. Many people on the street agree he should not be charged, as he was probably out of his mind with grief at the loss of his child."

"I don't believe it," Quinn said, sitting back in his seat and crossing his arms, angry about something that may or may not have happened over seventy years ago.

"Mrs. Anderson was understandably distraught when her husband was removed from their home as he had been caring for her after her loss. Neighbours came out to see what was happening and many of the women gathered around Mrs. Anderson, all speaking well of Mr. Anderson and assuring his wife they would help her through

this. What a terrible string of events to lose first your unborn child and then your husband."

"It's interesting," Phil said, "how the story is turning into a human-interest piece, as opposed to being strictly about a murder. I wonder if the reporter knew your grandparents and was trying to garner support for him. What was the reporter's name?"

Quinn looked at the headline. "Chris Hampton."

"Could be a woman, Christine," Ruth said.

"Oh, my listen to this," Ellie said. "It's from three days later."

"When the defendant, Mr. Anderson, appeared in court this morning to enter his plea of not guilty, the room was packed. Mrs. Anderson was sitting in the front, surrounded by friends and neighbours, some becoming loud in their disbelief of Mr. Anderson's guilt, requiring the Judge to have them removed from his courtroom. The Judge informed everyone to behave or he would have the room cleared. He then said that there would be a trial, wherein evidence would be supplied by the officers who handled the case. The Judge asked Mr. Anderson if he had a lawyer, to which the defendant replied he did not, as he was not guilty. Mr. Anderson was advised to get one, as the penalty for murder could result in the death penalty. Upon hearing this, Mrs. Anderson fainted in the courtroom and the room was finally cleared."

"Oh, man," Quinn groaned. "They didn't have the money for a lawyer. This was when they were first married, and my grandfather had a job as a train mechanic at Angus Shops in Rosemont. He wasn't making a lot."

"Oh, wait, wait!" Ellie said, grabbing Quinn's arm and digging her fingers in. "Listen to this! The next day's edition."

"What news to report! The police have released Mr. Anderson from custody and have given the following statement. "On this, the 15th of May, Mrs. Watkins appeared at the police station early in the morning and confessed to the murder of her own husband. She admitted she had suffered at his brutal hands for many years, and the last straw for her was the death of Mr. and Mrs. Anderson's unborn child. "I am at peace now," were her words as she gave herself up. We regret any

inconvenience to Mr. Anderson and have closed our case against him. He is free to return home." So, this reporter is happy to report that justice has prevailed."

"There's a picture!" Ellie's excitement was contagious, and she passed the laptop around to each senior so they could see the photo of Quinn's grandparents on the steps of the police station, hugging and crying as he was released.

"Justice certainly does prevail," Shirley said, wiping a piece of dirt from her eyes as inconspicuously as she could.

Quinn slumped back in his seat, shaking his head. "I had no idea."

"Why were your grandparents here in the first place?" Phil asked.

"Like I said, they met here." Quinn glanced again at the picture of his grandparents hugging and ran a hand over his face. "My grandfather was born here, first of his family to do so. And Gran loved it so much in Montreal, that when they married, there was no thought of going anywhere else. This became her home too."

"We know you grew up in Scotland," Norma said. "And you only met your grandfather a couple of times?"

"Well." Quinn sat forward and laced his fingers together. "My mom was their only child. Something went wrong during her birth and Gran couldn't have anymore children. Maybe because of the previous loss, but I'm not sure."

"That's too bad," Ruth said.

"But they had a wonderful life," he said. "I've seen the photo albums; they travelled a lot. And when my mom met my dad, who was visiting from Scotland, Gran knew my mom would never stay here. And she didn't. Within half a year, Mom had moved to Scotland and married my dad."

"And did your grandparents follow them over there?" Jeremy asked.

"No. They each had a group of friends, and full lives right here. But they went to Scotland a few times when all us kids were young. And then my grandfather died of a heart attack when I was about fifteen."

"So, your grandmother was all alone?" Ellie asked.

"She was, and she wasn't." Quinn smiled at her. "Like I said, she had an excellent group of friends and she loved her life here. She volunteered for tons of charity work and managed comfortably with my grandfather's pensions. Oh, and she tutored for a family for many years. They lived in Westmount, and she stayed in their carriage house. They appreciated her so much that they sold it to her once their children were grown."

"Oh, that's how she got that lovely little house!" Ellie said. "And now you live there."

"It's funny how many homes were demolished or renovated around her, but Gran's house stayed the same. She loved it. And my family came to visit her here, and she did get back to Scotland a few times."

"And what did she die of?" Ruth asked softly. "If you don't mind me asking."

"Not at all." Quinn looked at her and smiled. "She died the best way anyone could, in bed, at night, asleep. The doctors think it was quick."

"And are you going to continue living there?" Norma asked, side-eyeing Ellie to watch her reaction.

"Haven't decided yet." Quinn shifted in his seat. "For now, it's home."

"Damn!" Jeremy jumped up. "Quinn, can I have a word?" He disappeared inside the cabin.

Everyone looked at each other, eyebrows raised as Quinn got up to follow him.

Chapter Nine

Jeremy paced around the island in the kitchen. He threw up his arms when he saw Quinn, and whispered loudly, "I don't have a ring!"

Seconds later, the door banged open and Shirley headed straight to the sink. She washed her hands, but failed at being nonchalant about it.

The men stared at her, waiting for her to leave. But she didn't. She took a towel and dried each finger separately, looking from one man to the other, her eyes narrowing into thin slits.

"What's going on?" she asked.

Jeremy let out an enormous sigh. "It's a secret."

"It's obvious you're distressed about your secret, so maybe I can help."

Jeremy bowed his head and contemplated the floor before straightening his shoulders and facing his soon to be sister-in-law. "I'm going to ask Ruth to marry me today, but I don't have a ring. I want it to be a special moment and I messed it up before it even got started."

Shirley stared at him and a slow grin curled around her lips. In a split second, she was across the room and had Jeremy in a bear hug. "How wonderful! I'm so thrilled for you both!"

Jeremy returned the hug, then stepped back. "Thank you, Shirley. But I've still got a problem."

"Maybe we could borrow a ring," Quinn suggested.

"No," Jeremy shook his head, "I want it to be from me. Something old, or..."

"Let me think," Shirley paced the floor for a moment. "We know Ruth loves nature, so why don't we make her something and then you can get the real thing later?"

Jeremy nodded, considering the idea. "That just might work."

"Quinn," Shirley said, "do you mind if I take Jeremy off? We have some hunting to do."

Quinn motioned for them to be on their way. He followed them out of the cabin and watched them disappear into the woods, heads together, whispering.

Quinn joined the group back at the picnic table and heard the tail end of a story Norma was regaling everyone with.

"And so I said, if you can't find the number, you don't need a phone." Norma threw her arms wide as if delivering a punchline. The others laughed and, one by one, they all tried to outdo each other with terrible jokes.

Ruth patted the empty seat beside her and motioned for Quinn to sit down. "So, where did my sister and Jeremy go?"

Quinn, being quick on his feet, said, "Oh, Shirley wanted to show him a plant she wanted to identify and put in her landscaping catalogue."

Ruth gave him her teacher stare, but he refused to weaken and give up Jeremy's surprise.

"She's becoming quite the landscaper, isn't she?" Quinn asked innocently.

"She is," Ruth said, turning away from him. "But you're a terrible liar, Quinn Walsh."

***

Shirley led Jeremy down a well-trodden path, away from the cabin, and didn't stop until the voices of their friends in the distance were mere whispers in their ears. She turned to him, hands on hips.

"So, Mr. Jeremy Butler." She grinned at him. "Tell me exactly what you're planning and let's make sure this goes off without a hitch."

"You know, Shirley," Jeremy said, taking his time to find the exact words he wanted to say. "When I found out about what you had done all those years ago, my first thought was deep sadness. Not so much for us, but for you."

Shirley's shoulders slumped and her whole façade of excitement slipped. "I ... I...".

Jeremy held up a hand. "No, let me finish. All those crazy feelings I had at the beginning when you told me Ruth had married and moved away, all that hurt. And it took a long time to come to terms with that. But I found a lovely woman to marry, and we had Sam, who has been the light of my life all these years. I would never have had *this* Sam had Ruthie and I married, and the world would be poorer for him not being here."

Shirley reached out and Jeremy took her hand. "I'm so sorry, Jeremy."

"None of that!" Jeremy gave her fingers a gentle squeeze. "It's in the past. We are here now, and I'm an old man, Shirley. I am determined the last years of my life will be happy ones."

"And Ruth makes you happy," Shirley said.

"She has made me happy all my life, even without being with me."

"Right." Shirley snatched her hand back, turned away, and tried to hide the fact she was wiping a tear. She was becoming quite the weepy lady in her old age. But it startled her to realize how deep her love for her sister was, and how much she wanted Ruth to be happy.

"So," Jeremy said, being the gentleman that he was and ignoring her discomfort. "I'm taking Ruth out on a canoe ride to pop the question. I want to make a ring, but have no idea how to do that. What do you suggest?"

Shirley looked around at the vegetation, stepped towards some plants, reached for a flower, then shook her head no.

"Nothing fancy," Jeremy said, following in her shadow with every step she took. He reached down to push a plant away from a flower and jumped back. "Shirley, is this poison ivy? Leaf of three, let them be?"

She turned to the plant he was pointing at and then at his hand, held far from his body. "Oh, boy, did you touch it?"

"I grazed it, but..." he took a few steps back onto the path and kept his hand in the air.

"Okay, we'll deal with your hand in a second, trust me." Shirley frantically looked at the surrounding foliage. "You know what?" Shirley turned to him. "Ruth liked to take blades of grass and make a whistle out of them. How about we go minimalist, braid blades of grass tight and use that? Is that too simple?"

"That's perfect, Shirley." He watched her sort through the grass along the path, picking and discarding blades until she found enough to her liking. Within minutes, she'd created a delicate grass ring. "Will this do?"

"You really are good with plants." He smiled. He took a handkerchief from his pocket with his good hand and held it out. Shirley gently placed the ring on it, pulled the edges together, and replaced it in his shirt pocket. He gave it a pat.

"Now let's get back to the cabin and take care of that hand," Shirley told him as they headed back to the others. "I'm sure Norma has something in her bag of tricks that will help."

***

When they arrived, everyone was startled by their panicky looks.

"What's wrong?" Ellie asked. She jumped to her feet, ready for whatever had happened. She had never gotten out of the practice of being ready for anything as her daughter had been a daredevil.

"Jeremy touched poison ivy and we need to act fast," Shirley said. "Norma? What have you got for that?"

"Same thing as for the windshield wipers." Norma was up and moving to the cabin. "Come with me, young man. We'll get you sorted."

As they headed into the cabin, Shirley plopped down in her seat, a small bunch of flowers in her hands. "Would you look at these? Jeremy took some pictures for me, and I want to identify them when we get home. They'd be perfect for the Tiny House Haven entranceway."

Quinn gave Ruth an "I told you so" look.

"I didn't see any signs mentioning anything about poison ivy," Ellie said, frowning. "Did anyone else?"

"That should be at the reception desk, right?" Phil asked.

"I don't remember seeing anything," Quinn said.

The cabin door thumped open, and Jeremy and Norma rejoined them.

"How bad is it?" Ruth asked Jeremy.

"Apparently, if you get to it quickly, without rubbing it, the symptoms are diminished," he said. "As a matter of fact, I don't feel a thing!"

Norma sat beside Shirley and stretched out her legs. "If you attend to it within ten minutes, you'll be good."

"And I feel great." Jeremy walked over to Ruth and held out his hand. "Ruthie, would you like to go for a canoe ride with me?"

"Don't be daft," she answered with a laugh before noticing everyone had stopped to watch them. Tentatively she added, "I doubt either of us could *get in*, let alone *get out* of a canoe!"

"Well." Jeremy kept his hand out. "I've been in canoes all my life, and I think it would be a grand thing to do."

Quinn got up. "And we'll help you get in and out.

"Well." Ruth seemed to consider it.

Gripping her hand, Jeremy guided her down to the dock. Quinn hurried ahead of the couple, arriving first, handing out a lifejacket for Jeremy, and helping Ruth with hers.

"You know we can swim, right?" Ruth asked with a slight shake of her head.

"These are the rules," Quinn said, tightening the last strap and jiggling her lifejacket to make sure it was snug.

Quinn helped Jeremy in and turned to Ruth. She held his hand in a death grip and stepped in, immediately dropping to the seat, holding the sides tight with white knuckles as the canoe rocked. Quinn handed Jeremy an oar and gave them a slight push out into the lake.

Ruth dipped her hand in the water and smiled. "Oh, it's lovely."

Jeremy fumbled with the oar, wiped his hands on his pants, and put the oar in the water for the first stroke.

The rest of the group followed the goings on from their chairs near the fire pit. "I can't believe she's doing this," Norma said, shaking her head in amazement and admiration.

"Oh, just wait," Shirley whispered. "You haven't seen anything yet."

But what happened next, no one expected. Despite Jeremy's crisp strokes, and within a few feet of the dock, the canoe struck something and came to an abrupt halt.

"It's only a log," Jeremy shouted back to a worried Quinn and Ellie. Jeremy leaned forward and pushed against the log with the oar. The oar slipped from his grip and into the water. He reached out after it, leaning too far and too late to grab it. The canoe rocked and then tilted.

"Sit down, Jeremy!" Ellie yelled. "Sit down now!"

Too late. The canoe lost its ballast and tipped slowly to the side.

"Jump, Ruthie!" Jeremy yelled, grabbing her hand, pulling her from the canoe's path. With lifejackets on, they bobbed in the water as the canoe drifted towards the beach.

Without hesitation, Quinn and Ellie jumped in and swam to the seniors. "You'll be okay," Ellie said. She latched a hand around Ruth's lifejacket, and towed her to shore. Quinn was close behind with Jeremy.

"For pity's sake, Ellie," Ruth said, kicking her feet behind her. "I know how to swim."

When they crawled up on the beach, the group was waiting to help pull them out. Norma had raced back to the cabin the minute the boat tipped, and now her arms were full of towels. She tossed one to Shirley, who enveloped Ruth within. Jeremy was almost smothered when Norma wrapped a large towel around his head and shoulders.

"Jackets off," Quinn called to Ellie, as he unsnapped Jeremy's life jacket and pulled the towel more snuggly around him. Norma threw him another and Quinn layered it on top of the first one.

Ellie followed suit, and by the time Ruth was free and drowning in towels herself, her teeth were chattering.

"Right," Shirley commanded. "Back to the cabin and out of those wet clothes."

Everyone cleared a path, allowing the wet canoeists to hurry into the cabin, following behind.

"Come with me, Ruth," Shirley said in her no-nonsense voice as she pulled her sister into Ruth's bedroom and closed the door with a firm click.

Jeremy stood in the living room, water pooling at his feet.

"This way," Quinn said as he guided the older man into the bathroom. "Ellie, can you get some clothes for Jeremy, please?"

Ellie dashed into Ruth's room and returned minutes later with a dry set of clothes. Knocking on the bathroom door, she wiggled them through the slim opening and into Quinn's hands.

"We need some hot chocolate!" Norma declared before bustling into the kitchen.

By the time the swimmers were changed, Norma had a big batch of hot chocolate waiting. With mugs on the table and everyone seated, they waited for the others to appear.

Jeremy was the first to arrive, his hair all skewed from a quick rub down, but otherwise looking fine.

Ruth returned slower, her face pale, her eyes twinkling.

"What was he thinking?" Phil muttered. "They could have drowned!"

"The water *is* really warm," Ellie conceded as she came back from the larger bedroom, wearing dry clothes. She finished towelling off her hair while Quinn disappeared into the bathroom to change.

Ruth's lips were a faint shade of blue. Shirley grabbed a throw blanket off the couch and wrapped her sister in it before seating her at the table beside Jeremy. She pushed a mug of hot chocolate into Ruth's hands. "Drink this. It'll help warm you up. Jeremy, wrap your hands around your mug, dear." She found another blanket and tucked it in around his shoulders before finding her own seat. Her hands shook as she brought her mug to her lips.

And that's what Jeremy did. The heat from the mug and the warmth of the dry clothes and blanket soon had him warm enough to push the blanket down his arms. He took a mouthful and closed his eyes. "This is exactly what the doctor ordered."

Phil and Norma were already halfway done with theirs, Phil sporting a delicate chocolate moustache across his upper lip.

"Love the look, Phil," Jeremy said as Quinn joined them at the table. He motioned to his upper lip and Phil swiped it clean. "Ruthie," Jeremy continued. "Maybe we should go back home now. I don't know what I was thinking about asking you to do such a silly thing. I'm so sorry, but I can't let you get ill."

"Don't worry, dear," Ruth leaned into him. "Finish your drink. And we're not going anywhere. Norma hasn't found her buried treasure yet." She snaked an arm through his and pulled him close. "I'm fine," she whispered to him.

"This has been the most exciting trip I've had in years," Phil said.

"It is," Jeremy agreed, giving Quinn a quick shrug of his shoulder. "But I'm going to have a little lie down, if you don't mind."

"What a great idea." Ruth nodded. "I'm with you. I hope no one minds." She stood up and clutched at the blanket as it started to slip down her shoulders.

"Sounds wonderful." Ellie looked longingly at the futon in the living room area.

"And the rest of us," Norma said as she stood up and stretched, "will go looking for buried treasure. You don't mind missing it, Ruth?"

Ruth was halfway to her bedroom before she turned. "Not at all," she waved them off, her eyelids already drooping as Jeremy closed the door behind them.

"You don't think they're going to..." Shirley asked.

"Shirley!" Phil said, aghast. "Even if they were, it's none of our business. But from how tired they are after all this excitement; they'll be asleep the minute their heads hit the pillows. Now, are you coming or not?"

Phil led the way out of the cabin, and the rest trooped along after him.

"If I could only remember where I buried it," Norma mumbled to herself as she closed the door behind them.

Chapter Ten

"How are you going to dig it up?" Shirley asked Norma as she fell into step beside her. Norma reached the picnic table, then stopped.

"Um," Norma said as she looked around at the other cabins and the lay of the land. This whole adventure suddenly felt like a fool's errand. To even think she could find the jewelry after all these years was ridiculous.

"Here." Phil handed her a small gardening spade. "I found it beside the steps of the cabin. Will this do?"

"Thanks, Phil." Norma took the spade and continued her surveillance of the property. "I think we were staying in the next cabin over." She started walking towards the next building and everyone followed. "There's a good view of the owner's cabin from here, which is right next to the office."

She mounted the steps to the cabin her family had stayed in decades ago and checked the distance. "Yes, this is it. I had just come out on the balcony when Tommy ran out of the owner's cabin with something in his hands. He was casual about the whole thing, but he walked behind all the cabins and right into the spill-over cabin which is..." she hopped down the stairs and headed around the side of the building, "...right here."

"Wow, that is small," Ellie said as they stood in front of a tiny building that measured no bigger than ten by ten. There was a single window in the front beside the door, with a few rickety looking stairs leading to it.

"How could this be a separate cabin? It looks like a shed," Phil said.

"Big enough for two sets of bunk beds and nothing more." Norma peered through the window. "Still the same, I see."

"And where did he hide the jewelry?" Quinn asked, checking out the inside from over Norma's shoulder.

"In his pillow, of all places!"

"You were very brave to do what you did," Shirley said. She turned slowly, trying to picture how everything was placed. "You said everyone was at the beach playing games?"

"Yes," Norma came to her side and pointed. "But past the office, where the beach continues beyond. I'm quite surprised Tommy took the chance he did."

"Anyone could have seen him," Ellie said.

"Not really." Norma replayed the whole event in her mind. "It was game day. Once a week, on Wednesdays, the owners organized water games on the beach and everyone turned up. Winners got ribbons and small gifts, like candy from the office store. Some families would come year after year, like us, usually at the same time. We got to know a lot of people over those summers. Everyone was extremely competitive with the games, doing better than the Martins one year, and better than the Smiths the next. It was a matter of family pride. So, no one would have seen him. They would have been too intent on winning."

Norma took a minute and focused on the landscape. She gingerly stepped up onto the porch of the tiny cabin, testing each plank before putting her foot down. "I hope the Wagners fix this before more guests come! Okay. So, I came out of the cabin with the jewelry in a plastic bag."

"You put everything in a bag?" Phil asked.

"No, that's how I found them. I took a quick peek though. Inside the plastic bag was a cloth bag, and inside that was all sorts of jewelry."

"Did Tommy come out of the office with the jewels in his hand or already in a bag?" Quinn asked, his police training rearing its head as he pieced together the puzzle.

“I couldn’t tell from that distance.” Norma came off the porch as slowly as she had gone up.

“What did you do next?” Shirley asked. “And how in the heck did you know what to do in the first place?”

“I didn’t.” Norma turned to stare at the cabin and then let her gaze wander past and into the woods beyond. “I was acting on adrenaline. I knew I had to make sure nobody found them in his possession.”

“How did you decide where to bury them?” Ellie asked.

“I dashed behind the cabins, where no one could see me.” Norma headed that way and she heard the others following along. “There!” She pointed to a large tree sixty feet away. “I remember how huge that tree was and hoped it would shield me.”

They reached the enormous oak tree which was located in an open area. It commanded a large space and had two old wooden benches set up in the shade beneath. Shirley plopped down on one, and Phil sat beside her. “This is lovely,” Shirley said, craning her neck and looking up at the birds in the branches.

“Is the location around here?” Quinn asked, scoping out the ground.

“Well,” Norma stood near the tree and looked back at the cabins. “I think I was on the other side, away from everyone. I don’t remember the benches being near and I tried to get as far away as I could, but...” She moved around the tree and shook her head. “Everything looks so different,” she muttered.

Ellie gave her a quick hug. “It’s been decades, Aunt Norma. Maybe the bag is gone.”

“I hope not.” Norma pulled away and started pacing the area. “There was a large, flat rock on the ground and an indentation in the dirt alongside. I dug between the ground and the rock and found a cavity. I threw in the bag and covered it all up.”

Quinn strolled around, pushing grass aside and moving leaves and branches with his foot. “Here!” He waved at them from a few feet away. “How about this?”

Everyone hurried over to see a long flat rock three quarters covered with debris. Bending down, Quinn cleared the rock until it was fully revealed.

"Yes," Norma said. "This must be the place. Let me think." Her stomach clenched with nerves as she walked around the rock, bending down and clearing spots Quinn's foot hadn't brought to light.

"Where's the spot?" Shirley asked.

"Patience, Shirley," Phil told her. "Give her a minute."

"Patience was never one of my virtues," Shirley mumbled.

"But a kind heart is," Phil answered.

Ellie and Quinn turned to look at him, and Phil scowled and shrugged. "Did you find anything?" he asked sharply, trying to shift their focus from his slip of the tongue.

Norma dropped to the ground on her knees and pulled some weeds out from the side of the rock. Holding the spade in a death grip, she started digging. Dirt flew in all directions as Norma grunted at the effort she was making.

"Norma." Quinn knelt beside her. "Can I do that for you?"

"No, no," she waved him away. "This is something I have to do myself."

After a few more minutes of heavy breathing and struggling with the ground, she sat back, the spade limp against her knee.

"Maybe this isn't the right place," Ellie said gently, worried about her aunt working so hard.

"I'm sure it's not." Norma struggled to get up and Quinn reached for her arm and helped her to her feet.

"Okay," Phil said, walking around the tree. "Let's keep looking, dig a few more holes. We'll all take a turn."

Norma held up a hand and shook her head. "Thank you, guys, but I doubt the jewelry is even still here. And I'm sure the Wagners wouldn't be happy with me digging up their property."

"Norma," Shirley said sternly, catching and holding Norma's eyes. "This is not something to give up on. That's not like you. Certainly a few more holes won't be a big deal. If it bothers you so, go ask that delightful Mr. Wagner for permission first."

"I think you should ask *Mrs.* Wagner," Ellie said.

Norma looked at her friends' eager faces, each excited about the prospect of her finding something so many years after she'd buried it. This was an adventure for them all, and she refused to let them down.

"Okay." She passed the spade off to Phil and wiped her hands across the grass to remove whatever dirt still clung to her fingers. "I'll go speak to them."

"We'll meet you at the cabin," Shirley called after her, taking Phil's arm in her hand and leaning into him as they headed back.

Ellie and Quinn hurried to catch up with Norma. "Wait, Aunt Norma," Ellie puffed as she caught up. Maybe she was wrong about her aunt being the weaker of them. "We'll come with you."

"Let me do all the talking," Norma said as they pushed open the office door, hearing the bell tinkling as it closed.

Pounding footsteps came down the staircase once again, though slower, and with a definite pause between each thump hitting the next step. Mr. Wagner came into view; his wife was close behind.

"And how can we help you?" Anna asked them, a welcoming smile on her face that actually reached her eyes. Her husband appeared to have never learned how to smile. Not a good approach to a customer friendly business.

"Oh," Ellie butted in. "I was wondering why there's no poison ivy warnings around the camp? One of our group stumbled upon a plant."

"But we do..." Anna's eyes scanned the counter, then she knelt down to check underneath. She stood up with a dirty sign in her hand and slammed it on the counter in front of them. She turned to her husband and narrowed her eyes before continuing. "It would appear that whoever cleaned the office last misplaced the sign. My apologies. Is there anything we can do?"

"No, thank you," Ellie said, startled by the frustration coming from the woman. She did not envy Mr. Wagner after they left.

"Yes, well, I'm hoping you might help me with something else," Norma started, realizing how foolish she now felt about the whole adventure and dragging her friends into it. "My family spent every summer here and the last time we were here, I was about ten years old. I buried something precious to me and was sure we'd come back the next summer and I could dig it up. Such a silly kid thing to do, but sadly we never came back."

Ellie watched in amazement as her aunt wove a story of fiction that sounded real even to *her* ears, and *she* knew the truth.

"So, I was wondering if you'd allow me to dig a few holes around where I think I buried this item so I can find it again. It would mean a lot to me."

"No!" The word flew out of Mr. Wagner's mouth before Norma finished her request. "I'm sorry, but we can't allow every customer to go digging through the ground, leaving holes for people to fall into. And whatever this item was is probably not even there anymore."

Norma narrowed her eyes and gave him a steely gaze. "And how would you know that for sure?"

Mr. Wagner said something in German to his wife, his eyes never leaving Norma's.

"I'm sure you understand how..." Anna Wagner said in a calm voice, trying to lessen the harshness of her husband's tone.

"Oh, I assure you, Mr. Wagner," Norma never wavered from her locked gaze as she let a smile light up her face. "I am not crazy, but I thank you for your kind consideration."

She turned to go, then looked back at the couple. She rattled off a sentence in German and smiled at their stunned expressions before pushing past Quinn to get out of the office.

Ellie and Quinn caught up to her at the bottom of the stairs. "Wait," Ellie stopped her aunt from barreling down the path. "What did you say to them?"

Norma gathered herself, for she was clearly angry. "I told them they should be careful who they call crazy."

"Where did you learn to speak German?" Quinn asked, his curiosity on high alert. Something was up with Norma, and whatever it was, it was turning out to be quite interesting.

"Online," Norma said, then stormed back to the cabin.

Chapter Eleven

When Ellie and Quinn followed Norma inside, they found Ruth and Jeremy sitting cozily together in the living room. Everyone had claimed their beds and unpacked items they would need for the night. The cabin had a lived-in dorm atmosphere about it. As the temperature changed from warm to cool, the seniors bundled up in sweaters. Phil's had a strange-looking dog on the front, perhaps made for him by a relative. No one dared ask about it.

"Did you have a good rest?" Ellie asked Ruth.

Ruth's hand was in Jeremy's and if Ellie didn't know better, she'd swear they were glued together.

"We did actually, except for all the voices out back." Ruth raised her eyebrows in question.

Shirley took a seat in an armchair across from them and stretched her legs out with a groan of pleasure. "Norma was digging, but she didn't find the treasure."

"What did the owners say?" Phil asked Norma as she put the kettle on to boil on the stove.

"They would prefer that I did not dig up their precious ground," Norma said stiffly, still seething from being called crazy.

"Well," Jeremy said, "it *is* their property."

"Who's hungry?" Norma changed the topic. "How about some tea and cookies? I believe Maggie supplied some delights for us." She made a fair amount of noise as she opened cupboards to find the mugs.

"Chocolate chip cookies are good for whatever ails you," Ellie said as she took the large bag from the refrigerator and put napkins on the table for everyone. "We don't want anyone getting hangry."

"And how about another genealogy lesson?" Shirley suggested. "I quite like the idea of adding some background to our own stories. Finding others who came before us and all that."

"I have a suggestion," Ruth said as she spooned a small portion of sugar into her cup. "Why don't we try to figure out what types of occupations ran in our families. Did any of you follow in your ancestors' footsteps?"

"That's a great idea, Ruth," Ellie said before taking a quick sip of her tea. She brushed the crumbs from her fingers and booted up her laptop.

"But where would we find that information?" Phil asked. "We never talked about things like that in our family. We all knew what our dad did, but not granddad, or anyone before that."

"I know this one!" Jeremy's hand shot up as if he were in class waiting to be called upon.

They all laughed at his excitement.

"And what would that be?" Quinn asked, helping himself to a second cookie.

"Why census returns, of course!" Jeremy declared.

"That is one way." Ellie nodded. "But you can also check out newspaper obituaries, military records, city directories, wills, and local town histories, amongst others."

"And family stories, of course," Shirley added.

The clinking of spoons in cups and a few "Oh, my, these are good," comments took up the next few minutes. When the bag was empty and the last sips taken, everyone looked toward Ellie.

"Shall we pick someone and use them as an example? That way you'll know what to do for when we get home," Ellie suggested.

"How about Quinn?" Phil said.

"Oh, no," Quinn said quickly. "I've had more than enough excitement with my grandparents for a while, thank you very much. Plus, the newspaper article told us he was an engineer at the Angus Shops in Montreal, but I knew that already."

"Let's do Jeremy's family," Ruth said, giving him a smile. "What did your dad do for a living?"

"He was a postman," Jeremy said. "And it killed him."

"I'd think that would be a healthy occupation," Shirley said, puzzled. "All that walking and such."

"Walking in the day, drinking in the night."

"Oh, sorry," Shirley whispered.

"No worries," Jeremy said. "And his dad was a letter carrier. My dad told me they changed the name to postman in the 1880s. He *was* very proud of his job; I'll give him that."

Ellie's fingers flew across her keyboard. "Anyone want to hear a bit of history of Canada Post?"

"I knew you'd be an excellent teacher," Ruth said, settling herself in a comfortable position in her chair.

"I won't bore you, just share a few interesting facts," Ellie assured them. "It wasn't until 1908 that people living in rural areas had free delivery service."

"How was the mail delivered back in those days?" Phil asked.

"Let's see." Ellie scanned the article. "They would send letters and parcels between cities by train or even small planes, then they would use horse and carriage, and after that they used motorized vehicles. I remember when the postman came by every day to our door."

"And now we have to go pick it up at a community box." Shirley shook her head resignedly.

"But it's wonderful exercise," Phil reminded her.

She tiled her head, considering. "That's true."

"It always amazed me how they could carry those enormous packs on their backs," Ruth said.

"That's what got my granddad," Jeremy said. "His back gave out and my grandmother had to support the family. I never met him as he died rather young."

"So, your grandmother brought your father up alone?" Quinn asked. "Did your father have any brothers or sisters?"

"No." Jeremy shook his head. "Which was probably a great relief to my grandmother that it was only my dad and her to take care of."

"What was mail delivery like in Scotland?" Ellie asked Quinn.

"Well, I remember we had delivery twice a day," he said. "But that ended around 2004. My mother complained about it for months after."

"Twice a day," Norma said. "That's pretty nice."

"It used to be more than that in the old days," he said.

"Let's try something else." Ellie turned back to her computer. "I'm pulling up the 1901 census for Canada on the Library and Archives Canada site because it's free. I'll jump in and pick the Province of Quebec, District of Montreal and a list of pages has popped up. Let's pick one, the St. Laurent Ward, and open it. And here we have the column that says principal profession or trade. Let me read some of them to you." She took a breath and began, "Musician, brick layer, cook, tailor, office clerk, carpenter, plumber, stone cutter, undertaker."

"Oh, my!" Ruth said in surprise. "I did not expect *that* one."

"And all these people lived on the same street," Ellie said. "What a mishmash of people!"

"What's the most interesting occupation you've ever come across?" Phil asked.

"Well." Ellie thought for a moment. "I think it was my ancestor in Gloucester. He was a Verger and then a Beadsman."

"What's that?" Shirley asked.

"A verger is a lay person in a church who assists in religious services, and a beadsman, according to the dictionary, was someone who was paid to pray for someone. I'd never heard of a beadsman before. But the funny thing is, his father was a thatcher. You know those thatched roofs you see on cottages in England? That's what he did for a living. I guess his son didn't want to work with his hands."

"Or he was trying to better his lot in life," Ruth suggested as she stood up. "I'm going back outside to watch the wildlife and stare at the lake. Who's with me?"

It turned out that everyone was with Ruth, and they all found seats around the fire pit. The breeze was light and warm, and small mammals raced through the underbrush in the forest beyond. One inquisitive squirrel came out of hiding and took a few steps towards them. But when Quinn headed its way, it scampered off.

"I think I'll get this fire going for the BBQ," Quinn said as he used the sticks and logs supplied to build a fire worthy of a survivalist.

"Norma," Phil said, his knee jiggling up and down as he took a minute to phrase his next words. "You shouldn't let Mr. Wagner stop you from searching for the jewelry. We came all this way, and you deserve to find it."

"Stop pestering her, Phil," Shirley said. "She'll do what she wants. Now I'm getting a puzzle from the cabin and we can all put our heads together and do it in record time."

"Aunt Norma is a puzzle wiz," Ellie said. "You've been warned!"

***

Norma tried her best to live up to Ellie's belief in her puzzle skills, but her mind wasn't focusing. "Sorry everyone, I'm useless right now." She left the group working on it and went to help Ellie set the table for supper.

"Are you okay?" Ellie asked as she handed her aunt the plates. She caught the sigh that Norma tried to hide.

"I'm fine, dear." Norma put each plate down gently, as if struggling to do such a normal thing. "I'll admit I'm a bit disappointed, but let's just enjoy the rest of our time here." She refused to talk anymore about the buried treasure as she had convinced herself it was no longer there.

The door banged open and Quinn entered with a platter full of chicken wings and sausages, and an apology for the noise. He placed the food in the middle of the table. The others trickled in behind him and sat down.

"Can I help with anything else?" he asked Ellie.

"Here you go," she placed a large bowl of salad in his hands and took one last look around the kitchen before taking her seat with the others.

"A toast," said Jeremy, holding up his glass of water. "To Norma for having a great idea for a quick vacation, and to the kids for putting it all together."

"Who are you calling a kid?" Quinn asked, clinking his glass against everyone's before taking a sip.

"You're as young as you feel," Phil said, picking up a chicken wing with his fingers and taking a bite.

"Then I must be a hundred and forty," laughed Jeremy. "Okay, maybe only a hundred with the new knee."

"As long as you have something to look forward to each day, you'll be fine," Shirley said, helping herself to some salad and passing the bowl to Norma.

Jeremy stole a quick glance at Quinn and then over at Shirley. He wasn't sure how he would pop the question to Ruth now, but he wanted it to be somewhere special. But here in the cabin was not the place.

A knock on the door surprised everyone. Mr. and Mrs. Wagner poked their heads in. "Hello? Are we disturbing you?"

"Come in, come in." Ellie jumped up and met them halfway. "What can we do for you? Were we being too loud?" She said the last comment with a smile, but Ellie was not feeling too partial to Mr. Watner at the moment.

Mrs. Wagner gave her husband a jab in the ribs and he scowled at her. "I would like to apologize to you for my behaviour earlier." He looked straight at Norma. "It was not called for, and I was having a bad day."

Norma continued to chew and gave him a stare that would make a hit man quake in their boots. Then she smiled. "Not to worry, Mr. Wagner." She licked the chicken juice off her fingers. "Everyone has a bad day. But thank you for coming." She smiled again and returned to her meal.

The Wagners left quickly, Mr. Wagner almost running down the stairs with his wife closing the door gently behind her and hurrying after him.

Ellie glanced at her aunt and was sure she was the only one who realized that Norma's smile never made it to her eyes.

Chapter Twelve

As the meal wound down, Ruth jumped up and dashed into her bedroom. She returned with a camera and a smile.

"Excuse me!" Ruth said, catching their attention. "I've been messing around with the camera and I'd love to take some shots to document our vacation. Something for us all to look at later. Can I get a group shot of everyone at the table?"

She stepped back to the far wall and looked into the viewfinder. Slowly she raised the camera, finally standing on tiptoe. "I'm pretty sure I've got you all in."

Quinn jumped up and held his hand out for the camera. "Go sit, Ruth. I'll make sure no one gets cut out. You're more a part of this group than I am."

"Oh, well, okay." Ruth hurried back to her seat beside Jeremy and grinned as he put his arm around her shoulders and pulled her to his side.

Quinn fiddled with the lens. "Say family jewels!"

"Family jewels," they all cried out, huge smiles on their faces.

"Wait." Quinn held up a hand. "Let me take another, to be on the safe side."

A second round of "family jewels" was called out before Quinn checked the pictures and nodded. He handed the camera back to Ruth and resumed his seat.

"That was a good meal," Phil said, rubbing his belly. "Thank you, Quinn."

"My pleasure," Quinn said, finishing his salad and sitting back. "This has been a good day."

They were all quiet for a moment before Ellie stood up. "Dishes." She started gathering everything together. "Everyone out, I'll take care of this."

"I'll help," Ruth said.

Jeremy caught Quinn's eye and gave a nod towards the door. "Gentlemen, fancy an evening meander?"

"Sounds good," Phil said as he stood and pushed his chair in.

"And I'd like another go at that puzzle," Norma said.

"I'm with you there," Shirley said as the group headed out for their respective activities.

***

The light was fading as the guys followed a nearby path. The temperature was still above normal and the stars were beginning to appear.

"It's quiet, isn't it?" Jeremy said as they made a slow circuit of the cabins. Phil and he stayed close together, at times reaching out to steady the other.

"You mean without the women nattering away?" Phil asked, grinning to show he was kidding.

"Did you ever tell your wife that she nattered?" Quinn asked him.

"I'm still alive, aren't I?" Phil laughed. "And she was a delight to be married to."

"So, Jeremy," Quinn said, "what are you going to do about Ruth?"

Phil's head perked up, and he turned to Jeremy. "My gosh, did you lose the ring?"

Jeremy fished in his pocket and pulled out a damp handkerchief. Even after changing his clothes from their boating incident, he wanted it close to his heart. He opened it carefully to reveal a limp clump of interwoven grass. "No, it's still here, but I doubt it'll be useful at this point."

"You made her a ring?"

"Isn't that amazing?" Quinn said, kicking a stick out of their way on the path.

"I wanted it to be memorable." Jeremy tossed the clump to the ground. "But I guess I'll have to think of something else."

“You haven’t changed your mind, have you?” Phil asked, obviously worried that this was the case.

“Oh, no,” Jeremy assured him. “Not at all. But I want the proposal to be in a special place, and from the heart.”

“Ellie said that we’ll be stopping at a surprise location tomorrow on the way home,” Phil reminded him. “Maybe that will be a good spot.”

“Do you know where that is?” Jeremy asked Quinn.

Quinn held up his hands. “Not a clue. That woman is full of surprises, and I’ve learned in our short time together that things will be revealed when the time is right.”

“Not a pushy guy?” Phil asked. “She’s a wonderful lady, that Ellie is.”

“She is indeed.” Quinn nodded as they headed back to the cabin.

“And Jeremy,” Phil said. “You should make another ring. I think that’s the bee’s knees.”

Quinn grinned. He hadn't heard that expression in years.

***

“I’ll be done in a few minutes,” Shirley called from the bathroom as the guys walked into the living room.

Ruth and Norma were already in their pajamas, sitting at the table with their hands wrapped around mugs of hot chocolate.

Jeremy laughed when he saw Ruth’s cat pajamas and Norma’s Star Wars ensemble. “Well, ladies, you certainly are all the fashion tonight.”

“Is it bedtime already?” Phil asked, hiding an enormous yawn behind his hand.

“Oh, I’m ready. This fresh air will do it every time,” Jeremy answered. “Come on Phil, get your pjs and we’ll use my bedroom while Shirley hogs the bathroom.”

“I heard that,” Shirley called through the door.

"Any of that hot chocolate left?" Quinn asked as he peeked into the container on the stove.

"Plenty for all," Norma said, sending a half-hearted smile his way.

Ellie took a quick glance at her aunt before filling up a few mugs and bringing them to the table for the guys. She was forgoing a cup for herself, as chocolate in the evening would keep her up all night. She caught her aunt's eye and got a wink and a smile. But she knew something was bothering Norma, but didn't feel now was the time to bring it up.

"Did you guys have a pleasant walk?" Norma asked as Jeremy and Phil came out of the bedroom, wearing the same red and black checkered pattern pajamas. They both looked embarrassed.

Jeremy shrugged his shoulders and tried to make a joke. "Seems we bought at the same sale!" He looked down at his clothes and then over at Phil.

Shirley opened the bathroom door as they were passing and hid a smile, though her eyes popped wide in surprise. "You both look..."

"Like we should play checkers on their backs?" Ruth asked, giving Jeremy a quick kiss on the cheek as he sat beside her and took a sip of his hot chocolate.

Norma yawned, followed by Jeremy, Ruth, and Phil. Ellie and Quinn brought up the rear of the yawning domino effect.

Shirley finished her drink in a few gulps and took her mug to the sink. "Rinse and leave them for the morning, gang. I cannot keep my eyes open another minute."

"Thank goodness," Phil said. "I didn't want to be the first one to go."

"Come on Phil." Shirley put her arm through his and headed to their room. "It's been quite a day."

Against Shirley's suggestion, Ellie washed up the mugs, and Quinn dried them before putting them away. They listened to the last trips to the bathroom, the search for extra blankets, and a few coming back for glasses of water to put on their bedside tables.

Then the lights turned off, and it was quiet. Almost.

"Good night, Ruth," called Shirley from the other room.

"Good night, Shirley, sleep well," Ruth answered.

"Good night, John-Boy," Phil called.

"Good night, Mary Ellen," Norma joined in.

"Sleep well everyone." Ellie laughed, closing the bedroom doors and turning off the light in the kitchen.

"Is this what it's like having kids?" Quinn whispered.

"I heard that!" Shirley said.

***

Ellie and Quinn set up their futon bed in the living room, brushed their teeth and put on their own pajamas. Quinn returned to find Ellie on the edge of the bed, fidgeting.

"What's wrong?" Quinn sat down beside her and wrapped his arm around her shoulders.

"I'm tired, but I'm not tired, you know what I mean?"

"Same." He stood up and pulled her with him. He handed her a sweater, put his own on, and motioned to her shoes while he slipped into his. With a finger to his lips, he eased the front door open. Like children sneaking out of the house, they were down the stairs, along the path, and onto the dock.

They sat cross-legged and listened to the night creatures. The frogs were mesmerizing. The sun had gone down, but there was the faintest tinge of light to the west. There were no clouds, but stars kept appearing as the sky darkened.

Ellie leaned back and stretched out on the dock. Fireflies darted above her head. "This is so nice," she said, letting out a breath. "And yes, it's almost like having kids."

Quinn lay beside her, and reached for her hand.

"You've been unusually quiet tonight," she said.

He was silent for a moment. He brought her hand to his lips and kissed her fingers. "What you found out about my grandparents has left me a bit surprised and shaken, actually. I had no idea any of that had happened."

"I doubt it's something any family would want to talk about. But remember, the accusations were false, and they made it through, together."

"I can't imagine how my grandmother felt, what she went through, losing her child and almost losing her husband. It explains why they were so devoted to each other." He rolled over to her and brushed a strand of hair from her face, letting his fingers trace her cheek.

She turned to him and smiled. "This is such a magical place. I remember my dad talking about family vacations here, but it was only a story. Family was always so important to him."

"I remember when I was a kid and thinking I had too many sisters."

"Lucky bugger!" Ellie said. "I always dreamt of having brothers and sisters. I grew up with my cousin Sophie and her parents after my parents died, but that's not the same thing."

"And I always wanted to have lots of kids." Quinn watched her face, wondering what her reaction would be. "I think kids need siblings; you learn a lot from them. Right now, all I have are a bunch of nieces and nephews. Which is fine, but I hope one day to have my own."

Ellie remained quiet, her attention turning again to the stars above, her fingers squeezing his.

Chapter Thirteen

Believing her roommates were asleep, Norma climbed down the ladder from the upper bunk and tiptoed from the room. She closed the door behind her with a gentle click. She found the living room empty, and through the windows she noticed Ellie and Quinn on the dock.

The futon had already been made up for a good night's sleep, so she sank down into the armchair instead. What was she to do? Had she brought all these people here to help her on a fool's errand? And yet a part of her was sure she could find the bag she had buried decades before. She felt this was the time to make amends, no matter how anxious the whole adventure was making her. She was getting too old for this kind of excitement, and the accompanying sleepless nights and upset stomachs.

A picture formed in her head of the young girl who had loved to follow her around the cabins. Virginia had been shy, but so very curious. The day before the theft, Norma and Virginia spent an hour on the dock. There must have been something in the air that had both the girls chatting away, sharing hopes and dreams, as if they had been close friends all their lives.

And then Tommy's illness threw a wrench in all their plans, and the family left the next day. She hadn't thought about Virginia or the jewelry in years. The episode may have flitted across her mind when someone mentioned Tommy's name, but nothing more. But now the idea was firmly planted, and the Libra side of her demanded that she set the balance straight.

Her bedroom door opened a crack and Phil peered out. Seeing Norma, he joined her in the living room. "Can't sleep?"

"Guess it's too early for me," Norma joked.

"I doubt that." Phil sat on the futon and considered his words. "You want to continue digging, don't you?"

She nodded, one hand tapping on the arm of the chair.

"So, do it," he said.

Ruth and Jeremy, followed seconds later by Shirley, made their way out of their rooms.

"What's going on?" Shirley asked, blinking to adjust her eyes to the low light. "You guys talk really loud, you know that?"

"Norma wants to continue digging," Phil said.

"Are you sure?" Ruth asked.

"But imagine how good it will feel to return the family heirlooms!" Phil said. "You'll be righting a wrong."

"Where are the kids?" Jeremy asked, looking around for Ellie and Quinn.

"They're canoodling on the dock," Norma said, pointing towards the lake.

"They are *not* canoodling, Norma," Phil admonished. "It looks like they're talking and," he glanced closer at the young couple, "I think they're contemplating the stars."

"That's romantic," Ruth said.

"So, are we doing this?" Shirley asked, putting her shoes on as if the answer was already yes.

"Let me get some sweaters." Jeremy hurried back into his bedroom and returned with a sweater for Ruth and himself.

The others got theirs and once they were all warm and ready, met at the front door.

"Wait." Phil held up a hand. "We need flashlights."

Ruth went to the kitchen and pulled out each drawer until she found two big ones. She handed one to Phil and one to Norma.

"How did you know where they'd be?" Jeremy asked.

"Every kitchen worth its salt has a drawer with a flashlight," Ruth said, buttoning her sweater to the neck.

Norma reached for the doorknob and stopped, turning to her friends. "We have to be quiet and keep our flashlights pointed to the ground. We don't want anyone to suspect what we're up to."

"It's only 9:30," Phil said. "This is my grandchildren's bedtime."

"And us old people should be in bed at 8:30!" said Shirley

"Speak for yourself." Jeremy laughed.

With whispers and giggles, and a squeaky front door, they were soon outside and heading around the back to the gigantic oak Norma had shown them earlier in the day.

***

Quinn tapped Ellie on the arm and pointed. "Is that what I think it is?" he whispered.

Ellie turned to watch the seniors, one following the other, in their pajamas and sweaters, following Norma around the side of the cabin, the only light being the bobbing of their flashlights as they disappeared from view.

Ellie jumped up and followed, Quinn right behind her.

They heard the murmurs of quiet conversation as they rounded the building and saw the group off in the distance, huddled by Norma's tree, all of them looking at the ground as the beams of light played across the rocks.

Norma's light was moving erratically back and forth. "It's hard to tell in the dark," she whispered, "but I remember a huge rock, but there are three here! I couldn't see the office from the spot, and I remember *that* because I was terrified someone would catch me."

She stopped at one rock and looked up, noticing Ellie and Quinn for the first time. Norma nodded at them before getting back to the task at hand. She weaved her head from side to side to see if the upper floor lights in the office building were visible, then held out a hand to Phil. Like a surgical nurse, Phil took the flashlight from her and handed her the spade with a slap to her palm.

She began digging. The hard packed ground made the going tough. They all stood in the cool night air, watching Norma struggle.

Until Quinn held out his hand to Norma. She hesitated a second before handing him the spade. "We'll cover more ground this way," he said. "No pun intended."

"Voices down!" Ruth whispered from beside the tree. "I can hear you loud and clear."

"Sorry," Quinn mumbled as he jammed the spade into the dirt and eased it around.

"There's a slight indentation." Norma knelt at his side. She ran her hand along the outer edge of the rock and stopped. "Here, this crook here."

Even though Quinn worked the spade around the entire area, after five minutes, Norma had to agree it was not the right place.

"Almost done?" Ruth asked, her teeth chattering from the cold.

"Sorry, Norma, but I'm taking Ruth back," Jeremy said. "We'll wait for you inside. Anyone else coming?"

The rest shook their heads and Jeremy and Ruth headed back to the cabin; the beam of his flashlight barely noticeable.

Norma walked around the area again and then stopped. She looked at the office, down at the ground and up at the tree. "Here," she said. "I know it's here."

Quinn moved to the spot Norma pointed at and dug. The clink of metal hitting rock filled the air. "Damn, sorry."

Seconds later, the front porch light of the office came on. "Who's that?" Mr. Wagner called from the steps, as a bright flashlight beam swept the grounds. "Is somebody there?"

They froze, as if playing red light, green light, and not a sound was heard but the wind whistling through the tree branches.

Norma shivered.

"If somebody's out there, you better say so," came his voice, less loud than before. "I have a gun!"

And still they all remained quiet and in place.

"Damn animals," Mr. Wagner groused. "I tell you, Anna, this was a mistake. We need cameras!"

The door banged shut behind him and the group waited.

"Okay," Quinn whispered. "Let's get this done."

"SHHH!" Ellie said. "What's that?"

Something was on the path from the office. Something large.

"Hide!" With a quiet that belied their ages, each person found a nearby tree and hid behind it, facing away from the office. They held their breaths, stood as still as possible, and waited.

"You can come out," came a whisper on the wind. "It's okay, it's just me."

They poked their heads out, one by one, to find Anna sitting on the bench under the tree. When they all moved forward, she clicked on her flashlight and aimed the light at the ground.

"I can guess what you're doing, and I don't have a problem with it," she said, moving over to make room for anyone else who wanted to sit.

Shirley sat. "You're not going to turn us in?" she asked.

"Hardly." Anna laughed. "And don't worry about Otto coming out here. He hates the dark. But I walk the paths around the cabins each night to make sure everything is okay before going to bed. We've had someone break windows in one of the cabins, but I'm sure it was because Otto didn't pay someone's bill." She sighed.

"You need a dog!" Phil said.

"Otto is allergic. Please continue what you were doing. I'm as excited as you to see if your lost treasure is still here."

"Right." Quinn held up the spade. "Let's go."

Three holes and fifteen minutes later, they found the bag. Quinn dug a deep enough hole for everyone to see the crevasse. And to one side a hint of plastic flashed when Phil shone the light inside.

"There!" Norma hissed. "That's it!"

"SHHH!" everyone said to her at once.

"Sorry," Norma whispered.

Quinn maneuvered the space around the bag, digging the dirt loose and scraping it out with his hands.

"Easy there," Phil whispered. "Don't rip it."

Quinn pulled the bag out of the hole and held it up. The dirt of many years hid whatever the bag contained. He handed it to Norma.

"Now, let's get back inside," Shirley said. "I'm getting a wind up my sweater and it's not pleasant."

A blinding light shocked them all. Ruth had returned and now gasped as the flash from her camera lit the entire area. "Run!"

***

Norma had put her arm through Anna's and pulled her along behind them. And Anna seemed happy to oblige.

The single bathroom light was all they turned on as they gathered in the dining room. Norma set the bag in front of her, but Ellie grabbed a dish towel off the rack and handed it to Norma. "Let's not scratch the table."

"I was so worried Mr. Wagner was going to find us," Shirley said, plopping onto a chair and letting out a shaky breath. "Does he really have a gun?"

"He has a rifle," Anna said. "But he has no bullets and doesn't know how to use it. It's just for show."

"This is so exciting!" Ruth reached out and gave Norma's hand a quick squeeze. "I'm thrilled you've found it."

"And what exactly have you found?" Phil asked.

"Talk about having patience," Shirley joked.

"When was the last time *you* recovered stolen goods?" he asked her.

"I doubt any of us ever have," Shirley admitted.

Quinn raised his hand. "Guilty. I have, but never jewels."

Anna looked between them all, eyes open wide, not sure if they were joking.

Norma struggled with opening the bag until Ellie jumped up and got a pair of scissors and cut it open. Norma then untied the brittle strings of the cloth bag and emptied the contents onto the towel, gently separating the pieces.

"Wow," Jeremy said. "That's a lot more than I expected."

"To be honest," Norma said as she picked up a gold signet ring with worn out initials. "I never took the time to look at anything. I grabbed the bag, ran, dug a hole, and buried it all."

"Don't let Otto see this. He'll claim it belongs to him!" Anna said. "But where did you..."

"Long story short," Norma said, "they were stolen from the previous owner by someone I knew when I was ten. I buried it, planning to return everything, but life got in the way, and now I get the chance to do so."

"Wow," Anna said. "That's an amazing story."

Ellie reached for a string of slightly yellowish pearls and rubbed them lightly against her front teeth. "These are real, and they're beautiful."

"How did you learn to do that?" Quinn asked her.

"Google."

"Is that a diamond ring?" Ruth asked, pointing to a delicate ring in the middle of the towel.

Quinn picked it up and showed it to Ellie."Can you Google this?"

"Not if the diamond is in a setting of any kind," she shook her head. "For a lone diamond, you can fill a drinking glass three-quarters with water and drop it in. If it sinks, it's real."

"But how do you know so much about jewelry when you never wear any?" Shirley asked.

Ellie grinned. "I'm just curious, I guess."

"Norma," Quinn said, "I'm not a jeweler, but there could be a lot of expensive pieces here."

"I know there is." Norma sighed. "The owners made such a ruckus about the theft. For everything to be in such good condition after all these years, they'd have to be 14k gold or more. And I was sure they'd call the cops, and that's what made me do what I did. Like I said, I couldn't let Tommy get caught. He'd go to prison for sure."

"But he was ill, Norma," Ruth said.

"That didn't matter," Norma answered. "Look at all this stuff. This is a big deal."

Anna looked at the jewelry and sighed, her shoulders slumping.

"What's wrong, dear?" Ruth asked.

"Forgive me," Anna said. "I'm very happy you found what you were searching for and will return it. But I admit I was imagining how a windfall like this would help us stay afloat. But that is my problem to deal with. Maybe I should buy a lottery ticket!"

"Good heavens," Norma said. "You're not closing down, are you?"

"I don't want to sell." Anna shrugged. "I love this place and so does Otto, but he thinks we can do it all. With just the two of us, we're barely keeping things going."

"Why not hire help?" Phil asked.

"We've had to repair two roofs in the last year. We can't afford help."

"Not even local kids for minimum wage?" Shirley asked.

"Otto doesn't want strangers working here."

"So, it's only been the two of you for the whole five years?" Jeremy asked.

"Yes, well..." she sank back into her seat. "The first year was fine. But Otto has dreams we can't afford."

"Hence fixing up the owner's cabin to rent out?" Quinn asked.

"Yes."

"I'm surprised you supply linens," Norma said. "That's a nice perk. We usually all brought sleeping bags."

"That was Otto's idea, but he doesn't do the laundry. Most people do bring sleeping bags and their own pillows. But we've advertised the business as fancy camping, and we're stuck with that."

"Or you could offer a discount for people bringing their own sleeping bags," Shirley suggested, always the businesswoman looking for the best deals.

"When did you put heaters in the cabins?" Norma asked.

"The second year. What an enormous expense that was! But it's made customers' stays much more enjoyable, especially in the fall."

"So, why don't you open in the winter as well?" Phil asked.

"What? But the lake freezes over and..."

"Exactly!" Norma said, excited by the idea. "You could have ice skating or fishing. And set out cross-country ski trails or snowshoe paths, sledding runs down the hill. I know for a fact the hill at the back would be amazing for that. And it would be safe because you could groom it to run onto the end of the road. People could bring their own gear, and maybe you'd have a few old sets of skis or snowshoes for people to try."

"Oh, and have little gifts of marshmallows and hot chocolate waiting for guests in their cabins when they arrive," Ruth suggested.

"And I noticed you had a tractor, so adding a snowplow might cut down costs as opposed to hiring someone else to keep the roads clean," Quinn added.

"This is exactly the type of place people would love to come," Ellie said. "And maybe do something special for Christmas and New Year. Gear the holiday events to families so you don't have drunken youngsters spoiling all the fun."

"I've seen drunken adults do the same!" Phil said.

Shirley nodded. "True."

"Or you could have the road plowed by someone the first year, to see how it works, *then* invest the next winter," Quinn said.

"Otto likes to have a rest period when we're closed," Anna explained.

"From what I've seen," Shirley said, "Otto wants to make money. So, you close the camp in November, do a huge clean up and prep for the winter season. Close again in April and do the same for the summer period."

Anna's eyes were sparkling with excitement. "You know what? This could work. I love these ideas."

"And you pretend the ideas were all yours, Anna," Shirley said. "See what he says. You could make enough money to have that extra help you need. There are always students looking for part-time work, and even retirees who'd love working out in nature like this."

"Go speak to the town office and find out if you'd need any other permits and such," Ellie said. "I bet they wouldn't mind having more tourists around during the winter months either."

Anna jumped up, revitalized. "Thank you so much for all these amazing suggestions. I'm going to finish my walk and put this all on paper before bringing it to Otto. He likes to have plans in front of him."

Shirley got up and gave her a surprise hug as everyone else said their goodbyes. Anna headed home, a bounce in her step.

Phil covered his mouth as he yawned. "So, what's next?"

Norma gathered up the jewelry and returned them carefully to the cloth bag. As she tried to retie the strings, they fell apart in her hands.

"Do you want me to keep that for you, Norma?" Quinn asked.

"No, thank you." Norma stood up. "I'll stick it under my pillow. I trust you all, but if anyone else tries to steal from me, I'll smack them silly. Sleep well everyone."

Chapter Fourteen

Ellie was curled up with Quinn on the futon when a bedroom door creaked open at six thirty the next morning. The sun slipped through the living room window, skirted across the futon and landed on her shoulder. Its warmth made her smile. Someone whispered, "Sorry," from above. She squinted to see who was there.

Norma tiptoed past to the bathroom and closed the door gently behind her.

Quinn cranked one eye open and slammed it shut as the bright light registered. "It can't be morning already." He shifted on the bed, stretching out his body but making sure Ellie stayed glued to his side with an arm around her.

"How did you sleep?" Ellie kept her voice soft, not wanting to wake anyone else.

"Let's not ruin a lovely morning with complaints about how my back feels like a pretzel."

"I was worried about the length of the futon when we opened it."

"I almost envy you being so tiny." He turned to her and gathered her close, planting a light kiss on her lips, then pulled away with a start when the bathroom door opened.

"As you were," Norma muttered. "I'm setting up some coffee."

"That sounds great, Aunt Norma," Ellie said, sending her a sunny smile as the older woman passed them, averting her eyes.

"It's not like we're naked," Quinn whispered into Ellie's ear.

"No, but I don't think she wants to know that you're sleeping in your skivvies."

“I better get dressed.” Quinn threw back the covers and grabbed his pants from the chair. “We can’t distress anyone else this morning.”

As Ellie dove under the blankets to dress, the bedroom door opened and Ruth and Jeremy poked their heads out.

“Oh, good,” Ruth said, dashing for the bathroom. “We were worried you wouldn’t be up yet.”

“Be quick, my dear,” Jeremy said, as he started the dance of the full bladder, moving from one foot to the other.

Shirley was the next one to rise, and she joined the line behind Jeremy, banging on the door. “Ruthie, for the love of Pete, hurry up.”

Ruth was out in a minute, and Jeremy dashed inside. By the time he was done, Phil was in line for his turn. Quinn disappeared outside and returned with a raised eyebrow at the dwindling line.

Ellie folded the blankets for the futon and Quinn helped her return the bed back into a couch. “Feel better?” she said under her breath.

“There’s nothing like the outdoors for doing what must be done.”

“Really, Quinn,” Shirley said as she passed them, “you’re not a child. Surely you could have held it a little longer.”

“That’s what nature is for, Shirley,” Phil said, as he joined them in the kitchen.

“Nothing wrong with using mother nature once in a while,” Norma said from the kitchen. “When needs must, and all that.”

Ellie settled into the kitchen to make breakfast. “I’ve brought the fixings for pancakes and fruit, and Norma’s made coffee. This will take a few minutes, so you might as well relax for a bit.”

The sound of banging pots filled the cabin as Ellie read and reread the instructions on the pancake mix before beginning to put it all together. Norma and Quinn exchanged a glance. They were both aware Ellie was not the best at cooking, but were willing to let her have a go.

Quinn carried mugs and fixings for coffee to the table and waited for everyone to sit down before joining them.

"Have you decided what you're going to do, Norma?" Jeremy asked.

Norma knew what he was talking about, but didn't answer right away.

"Are you going to keep everything?" Shirley asked.

"Hardly," Norma said with a heavy sigh. "I'm still worried I might be liable in some form."

"Did you think about that before?" Phil asked. "Maybe finding the jewelry wasn't such a good idea."

"Maybe not," she agreed.

"Aunt Norma," Ellie said as she flipped a pancake over without dropping it on the floor. She smiled with delight. "We should try and find Virginia. I doubt she'll want to press charges once she hears the whole story. Chances are she's still alive. And perhaps the Wagners have some way of locating her."

Norma closed her eyes as if to gather strength. "I'd prefer not to speak with them again."

"He did apologize," Ruth pointed out.

"He did," Norma said. "All right. I'll do it after breakfast."

"And you know, Aunt Norma," Ellie said as she brought a huge platter of pancakes to the table, "we can always go looking for her in the records."

"Why does it sound like the word *records* is capitalized when you say it?" Ruth joked.

"Because it is, or should be," Ellie said as she sat down beside Quinn. "In my line of work, records are the holy grail."

"What exactly do you do?" Jeremy asked, looking ashamed he didn't know the answer.

"Besides teaching this group how to write their own stories..." Ellie began.

"Memoirs," Shirley butted in. "We're writing our memoirs."

"I like that better," Phil agreed.

"Fair enough." Ellie put a pancake on her plate and reached for the butter. "I also help clients set up their family trees, I do specific research for people, visit archives and graveyards, my personal favorite, and I write books for people who are starting out in their family history searches."

"And don't forget about the books you write for children." Ruth raised a fork and pointed it for emphasis. "I've read those and they're very good. I think a few adults would find them useful as well. You never talk down to kids, and that's great."

"And you earn a living this way?" Jeremy seemed impressed.

"I do," Ellie answered. "And I'm taking some courses about DNA and how to apply that. I'm a little late to the game on the whole DNA boom."

"I'm surprised you haven't done that already," Norma said.

"You know me, Aunt Norma." Ellie smiled at her. "I don't enjoy change, even when it's for the better."

"That's a fact," Norma muttered. "And it will be your downfall one day."

"That's a bit harsh," Quinn said.

Ellie had shifted in her seat, uncomfortable with where the conversation was heading. "Yes, well, nobody's perfect, but I try."

"Considering how long it's taken you to get back into life after Adam and Winnie died..." Norma started.

"Norma!" Ruth exclaimed. "That will be quite enough. Everyone gets there in their own time. And you should talk. You were only fifty when your husband died. Why haven't you found someone else?"

"I'm quite happy on my own, thank you very much," Norma said quietly, avoiding everyone's eyes.

"*I'm* not," said Phil and focused on his plate as he realized what he had said.

Ellie put her knife and fork down and looked at her friends around the table. "I want to share something with you all."

She had their attention.

"I think it's taken me this long to get, to coin the phrase, back to the living, because I felt guilty about the accident that killed Adam and Winnie."

"You weren't driving the car that hit them," Shirley said.

"No, but..." Ellie hesitated, then continued. "Adam and I had a big argument before they drove off. I can't remember what it was about now, but at the time, we were both ticked off at each other. It was so bad that we didn't even kiss good-bye. It's quite possible that he wasn't paying attention like he should have."

"And it's quite possible," said Quinn, "it wouldn't have made a difference."

"And you'll never know for sure," Norma mumbled.

"That's true, Norma," Ruth said. "But Ellie, you can't let it eat at you."

"That's what I'm saying though," Ellie said, a smile lighting up her face. "It's taken a while for me to understand that. I mean, *really* understand that. Survivor's guilt is a horrible thing. I wanted to hurt for as long as I could because ... I didn't want to forget them."

"Oh, dear." Shirley put her hand on Ellie's and squeezed it so tight that Ellie grimaced.

"Do you worry that you will forget them?" Jeremy asked, his fork paused in mid-air as he waited for her answer.

"No. That will never happen," Ellie said. "And they'd be so angry with me for wasting away and not wanting to rejoin the living."

"Winnie would have harsh things to say to you." Ruth nodded. "She had a way with words."

"She did," Ellie smiled, remembering how she and Winnie had discussed how Winnie should use her language properly.

"And now you're ready to continue living?" Quinn asked, not looking at her and holding his breath for her answer.

"I am." Ellie leaned over and kissed him on the cheek.

Everyone applauded.

"Hooray for the love birds," Norma said as she stood up and took her plate to the sink. "I'm off to speak to the Wagners. Wish me luck."

"Wait," Shirley said, scrambling up from her seat to follow. "I want to see Mr. Wagner in action. I'll be your bodyguard."

“What would I need a bodyguard for?” Norma said as the two women walked out of the cabin.

“I watch too many movies.”

“You do.”

Chapter Fifteen

The bell jingled above the office door when Norma and Shirley entered. Noises from above alerted them that someone was up and moving around, but it took a few minutes for anyone to appear. This time it was Anna, hair pulled back in a messy ponytail, and a raggedy sweater over a pair of paint-stained jeans.

"So sorry to keep you waiting," she huffed her way down the stairs and met them at the desk. "We are getting ready to paint the second bedroom upstairs, hopefully before all the guests arrive later today. We're planning to move in soon."

"Have you shared your ideas yet? Shirley asked.

Anna looked over her shoulder, lowered her voice, and shook her head. "I want to meet with the town office and make sure I have all the information we need before I give him the PowerPoint presentation."

"He'll never know what hit him!" Norma said with a grin.

Otto's entrance from the back room interrupted any further talk. A huge smile appeared and he spread his arms wide. "Is this not a wonderful fall day? I believe the trees will start changing color this weekend, and we are booked solid for the next week before we close for the year."

"I'm sure everyone will enjoy the beauty of nature," Norma said, forcing a smile in return. What was it about this man that annoyed her so much?

Otto inserted himself between his wife and Norma and took over the conversation. Anna gave the back of her husband's head a chilling look and raised an eyebrow at Norma.

"How can we help you?" Anna moved closer, ignoring her husband.

"I was wondering if you have the contact information for the previous owners," Norma said. "When I came here in the 50s, it was owned by Virginia's parents. They named the place after her, actually. But I never knew their last name."

"I do not know who the owners were," Otto said, folding his arms across his chest as if he had nothing more to say on the matter. "We dealt with an agent, never met the owners."

Anna held up a hand. "I remember that it was the original owner's son who sold it, though. But I don't remember anything else." She sounded sorry that she couldn't help them.

"That's a shame," Shirley said, watching Otto closely. "Are you sure the name wasn't on the listing or something?"

Otto moved his gaze to Shirley, and she stood her ground. "As I said, we left everything in the hands of the agent. Now, if you'll excuse us, we have to get back to work."

He motioned for his wife to proceed him and started following her up the stairs. He turned. "And don't forget that checkout time is at noon. Leave the key on the table. We hope you enjoyed your stay."

Norma ushered a stunned Shirley out the door.

"Can you believe that?" Shirley asked. "I mean, he should not be in this kind of business if he's going to behave so..."

"Unsociable?" Norma filled in the word for her.

"Exactly." Shirley shook her head. "That man has no social etiquette at all. Poor woman."

"I think she'd surprise you," Norma said as they walked down the road. "There's a strength about her I quite like."

***

Upon returning to the cabin, they found the others settled in comfy chairs, facing the lake again. Quinn had found a few fishing rods under the porch and was digging near the stairs for anything he could use as bait.

"You'd think they'd provide us something," Jeremy said as he took a rod and set the line out with a hook at the end.

"Here you go." Quinn handed him a worm, which Jeremy expertly attached. Quinn dug a few more. "Coming Phil?"

Phil looked at the lake, then at the rods. "I've never fished before."

Quinn grabbed one of the life jackets from under the table and helped him into it, juggling the worms in his hand. "This will do just fine." He handed Phil another rod, picked up his own, and they followed Jeremy onto the dock.

Phil shuffled towards them, taking one step onto the rocking dock and then he stopped. He was in distress.

"You can do it, Phil," called Shirley from her seat. "I bet you're the only one who catches anything!"

With her encouragement, Phil stepped closer to the edge, but decided fishing from the middle of the dock would suit him fine. He fumbled with the worm, but baited his hook and watched as Jeremy and Quinn cast their lines in on opposite sides. Then he cast his right into the middle of the lake, or so it seemed.

"I've missed this," Jeremy said, pulling his cap down over his eyes. "A quiet morning, calm lake, amazing weather, and good friends. Can't get better than this."

"Oh, I bet it can," Quinn teased him.

"She hasn't said yes yet." Jeremy gave a tug at his line, but nothing was biting.

"That's because you haven't popped the question yet," Quinn said. He was having no better luck with his own rod.

"I guess the canoe ride wasn't such a good idea after all," Jeremy said.

Phil froze. "But Jeremy, Ellie said we're stopping someplace special on the way home. I bet it will be a perfect place to propose."

"That's the plan." Jeremy yanked his line in to see the worm had disappeared. "Ah, well, it's the thought that counts."

"Whoa!" Phil cried out, pulling back hard on his rod. "I think I've got something."

Shirley led a slow charge of the women from their chairs down to the dock at Phil's cry. "Have you got one, Phil?"

They all watched the battle playing out in front of them as Quinn went to help Phil. "I've got it," Phil insisted, teeth clenched with exertion.

"Reel it in a bit, let it go, reel it in, let it go," Jeremy coached him. "It's like a cat-and-mouse game."

Within minutes, Phil had landed a decent sized lake trout and was holding it up by the line for his friends to see. "I did it!" He beamed.

Ruth pulled out her camera and aimed it at the fishermen on the dock. "Move closer together, you guys. This one is for a frame." She clicked a few shots and everyone clapped.

Phil started fretting. "I don't want it to die. How do I get it off?"

"Here." Shirley stepped forward, took the fish from him, carefully removing the hook from its mouth and released it back into the water. It remained in place but seemed to hold its own. "See, it's fine." She washed her hands in the water and held out a hand to Phil. He helped her up and together they peeked over the edge and watched the trout slowly swim away.

"That was amazing!" he said.

"Shirley is great at things like this," Ruth told him, giving her sister a warm smile. "I, on the other hand, only cook the catch, while Shirley is the hunter."

"Dad used to love to fish, and we'd take our time after a hard day of work on the farm and try to catch supper," Shirley said.

"We did eat a lot of fish!" Ruth laughed. "And the occasional rabbit."

"Dad caught those," Shirley took a deep breath. "I never could kill a furry animal."

"You always were a big softie," Ruth said.

Jeremy had taken his shoes off during this conversation, and rolled his socks up inside them before lowering himself to the dock, with Quinn's help. "Come on Phil, dip your toes in."

Everyone assumed it would be asking too much of Phil, but he was barefoot and easing down to sit beside Jeremy before anyone realized he was doing it.

"Oh, my, that's cold!" Phil squeaked, pulling one foot out and letting the toes of the other skim the surface.

"Leave them in for a minute, Phil," Jeremy advised, pulling his feet out of the water in front of him and dropping them back in. "It takes a couple of minutes, and then you don't feel the cold at all."

"More like they've gone completely numb!" Norma said. "But we're proud of you, Phil. This is a big step."

"Now I'm a man!" Phil joked, though something in his eye caught Norma's heart.

"You know what makes you a man?" she asked. "Only the body you were born with, and even that can change. Everything else is a human condition. I feel sorry for youngsters these days, all these ideas of what it takes to be this or that. Everyone has fears, and you either get over them or you deal with them, and that's just who you are. Gosh, why can't people just be themselves?"

The group was quiet, taking in Norma's speech.

"Shirley?" Phil got her attention. "Do you like to swim?"

"I do indeed," she replied. "Ruth and I sometimes go to the pool in town."

"Would you be willing to teach me?"

"Oh." Shirley seemed at first taken aback, then pleased. "I would be honored to do so, Phil. I think you'd quite enjoy it."

A gust of wind caused their fishing rods to roll close to the edge of the dock, but Quinn grabbed them before they ended up in the water.

"It's getting too windy for me down here," Norma said. "Ellie, what do you say we try to find Virginia? I need to return her mother's jewelry to her."

"Sounds like a plan, Aunt Norma," Ellie said, while Quinn assisted Phil and Jeremy. As a group, they headed back to the cabin, Phil and Jeremy still barefoot, swinging their shoes in one hand, their fishing rods in the other.

Chapter Sixteen

"I wish I remembered what Virginia's last name was," Norma said, shaking her head. "We'll never find her now."

"Ha!" Ruth said from her seat across from her. "Ellie can find anyone."

The friends were sitting around the table, cups of tea before them, each eager for what they would learn this time.

Ellie held up a hand. "I can't guarantee that, but there *are* a lot of ways to look for her."

"Facebook?" Phil asked. As Phil had gotten comfortable with the group, he had also taught himself how to use technology, and had joined Facebook to stay in touch with family. Now he believed Facebook was the best thing since sliced bread.

"Not to start with, Phil." Ellie smiled at him. She had a pad of paper on the table and her pen was tapping a rapid tattoo against it. "We're going to list the things we want to find and figure out ways to get the answers. Aunt Norma, what do you want to find most of all?"

"Virginia," Norma answered without hesitation. "I'm not even sure she's still alive! But if she is, she's the one who the jewelry should go to."

"Didn't Mr. Wagner say that it was the previous owners' son who sold them the business?" Shirley asked. "Wouldn't that mean there's a brother?"

"He wasn't around when I was here, so he must be a lot younger," Norma said. "Right now, I'd like to find Virginia, please."

Ellie put pen to paper and jotted that down. "And we don't have her last name, so that's what we should focus on first."

"You're not actually a magician, are you?" Jeremy joked.

"Her mind works outside the box," Quinn said from his spot on the couch.

"All genealogist's minds work outside the box." Ellie smiled at him. "We are an interesting breed."

"You'd make a good detective," Quinn said.

Ellie gave him a delighted smile. "From you, that's a compliment."

"So, how do we find the last name?" Norma asked, being as patient as possible.

"One thing we know for sure is that they owned this business, Virginia's Cabins," Ellie replied, scribbling on the pad. "So, let's see what we can find out about the business itself. There must have been advertisements for the cabins, so let's start with Google."

"It could also be in newspapers," Ruth said.

"It could," Ellie agreed, typing rapidly on her laptop. "But I want to check this first, and then we'll go that route."

"I never thought of Google as a genealogy tool before," Jeremy said.

"Oh, yes, indeed." Phil leaned around Shirley to talk to Jeremy. "I've found a lot of interesting things on Google. It often leads to other entries, some through the big guns, like Ancestry, but I found an article about a cousin in a local newspaper through Google. I would never have seen that. That paper isn't in Ancestry's collection, nor on Newspapers.com."

"Here we go," Ellie said. "There's an entry for the website of Virginia's Cabins, so let's find out what it holds."

Everyone waited patiently while Ellie scanned the page. "There's a drop-down page for the history of the place, but it seems the Wagners have updated the site and they only state that it opened in 1950. They don't mention the previous owners at all."

"That must be Mr. Wagner's doing." Norma snorted in disgust. "What a horrible thing to do, erase a family's business like that."

"I bet he changes the name altogether one of these days." Shirley shook her head in disbelief.

"So, let's go to another entry on Google," Ellie said, scanning the list.

"What about the images, Ellie?" Ruth suggested. "Maybe there's something there."

Ellie glanced up from the laptop at Ruth and grinned. "Oh, you're getting good at this! Okay, here we go. Bingo! Newspaper advertisement." She enlarged the photo and turned the computer around for everyone to see the screen.

"That's very nice," Jeremy said. "And it has the owners' names!"

Ellie turned it back around and read the advertisement aloud. "It's dated May 25, 1969, and it says *Virginia's Cabins, opening on June 1st, 1969, for another season of fun for the whole family. Myra and Albert Hamilton are happy to announce the addition of a fifth cabin for the coming season.*"

"Hamilton," Norma repeated to herself. "Now I remember. Yes! Virginia Hamilton. That's amazing, Ellie!"

"Now, how do we find Virginia?" Shirley asked.

"It's too easy to make assumptions," Ellie warned. "Like believing they lived around here because they owned this business, so we have to consider they may have lived further afield."

"It's time for the census return search!" Phil said. "You know why?" He looked at the others, not expecting or waiting for an answer. "Because we've got their first names and it will be easier to locate them."

"The pupil becomes the teacher," Ruth said to him.

Behind his hand, he whispered to her, "I'm really enjoying this."

"No need to whisper," Shirley said. "I think we can all admit that we've been doing some family searching on our own. It's great to write our own stories, but I am fascinated with finding out about my ancestors." She turned to Ruth. "Remind me when we get home to tell you about mom's mother. I found something very interesting."

"I can't wait," Ruth said.

"So, Norma," Ellie said, refocusing their attention back to the mystery at hand. "You said you were here in what year, and you were how old?"

"It was after the war, around 1946, and I was ten."

"And how old was Virginia then?"

"I would say eight or nine," Norma closed her eyes for a minute. "She might have been my age, but she was a tiny thing, which led me to think she was younger. I feel horrible that I never asked her."

"So, that puts her out of the 1921 census, but her parents could be there, so let's check that out," Ellie said.

"Library and Archives Canada again?" Ruth asked.

"Ancestry this time," Ellie said.

"Oh, I forgot to tell you," Norma said excitedly. "I got in touch with the library in town and we can use their computers to access Ancestry for free! They have a senior's plan with all sorts of perks!"

"Really?" Phil's eyes popped open wide, and everyone could see the wheels turning. "That'll be helpful."

"So," Ellie said as she accessed the site. "I'll go through the card catalog, use Canada as a keyword, and choose census and voter lists from the column on the left, and pick the 1921 census. Now, I'll put in Albert Hamilton's name, and Myra as his spouse." She hit the enter key and waited.

Ellie glanced over at her aunt and noticed the white knuckles wrapped around her tea cup. Ellie caught her eye and gave her a wink. Norma let her breath out slowly, and the color seeped back into her fingers.

"Well," Ellie said, "there's an Albert Hamilton in Amherst. And his wife's name is Myra."

"Which is only a few miles down the road from here!" Shirley said in surprise.

"This campground is northwest of Amherst, but I'm sure it would be in that census location. Hang on." Ellie opened up the page and scanned it. "I'll pass this around in a second, but Albert and Myra had no children at this time, and it says his occupation is carpenter."

"Not owner of a business?"

"He's only twenty years old here in 1921, so by the time he had this place, which was 1940, he would have been about forty."

"And this census was right after the first world war," Jeremy reminded them. "So, he may have served."

Ruth took his hand and held it tight, knowing how the memories of his own service in that war still haunted him.

"How old was Myra?" Norma asked.

Ellie returned to the screen and double checked. "Young. She was only eighteen in this census. Here."

The computer made its way around the table, each one taking a quick look at the information before sliding it to the next person. When it reached Ellie again, she jotted down another note on her paper.

"So, now that we have Virginia's last name," Ellie spoke to Norma, "it's time to look for a marriage for her. We have an approximate date of birth and her parents' names."

"Don't we need to know where she got married?" Quinn asked. He had been watching Ellie the whole time, but her concentration had never wavered.

"We have a lot of information right now and I'm going to assume." She held up her hand. "I know, I know, I'm the one who says never assume. But hear me out. Her parents were in the 1921 census in this area. The business is in this area. So, I'll *assume* Virginia was raised around here, and more than likely born here as well. At least let's start with that premise."

"Ancestry again?" Phil asked.

"Yes," Ellie answered. "But let me show you another way to search." She swung the laptop around and worked from the side so she could show them all the steps. "At the top menu, we hit the search button. I'm going to enter all the information we have in the query boxes that pop up underneath the top menu. We'll leave the date of marriage blank because we don't have that, and hit the magic button."

The group's patience was commendable, though Phil squirmed in his seat as the answers to the mystery unfolded.

"There is a marriage record for Virginia Hamilton marrying a Thomas Fortin in 1970. And..." She leaned closer to the screen. "Her father is noted as Albert Hamilton, business owner of Amherst, Quebec."

"Bingo!" Norma jumped up and clapped her hands. "We found her!"

Ellie grinned at her aunt and watched her do a little dance before sitting down, out of breath.

"What now?" Jeremy asked, as excited as the rest of them were.

"I hate to say this," Ellie said with a frown, "but I think we should search for her death."

"Newspapers." Phil nodded in understanding.

Ellie's fingers flew across the keyboard and she hit the enter button with a bit more force than necessary. "I'm hoping we don't find her."

The only sound was Phil slurping the last of his tea. "Sorry."

"Nothing under her married name," Ellie said as she returned to typing and waited. "Nope, nothing under her maiden name, either."

"Don't forget Find a Grave," Ruth said.

"On it." Ellie loved how the group was learning and remembering ways to find people. "Nope, she's not here either, under either name."

"They could have moved, though, right?" Shirley asked.

"They could have," Ellie agreed. "But I left the location field empty and no one by her name is listed anywhere."

"Wait," Norma said, leaning on the table towards her niece. "Google her with her married name."

Ellie smiled and returned to the laptop. "Well, well, well."

"What? What?" Norma asked. "Jeesh, Ellie, this is getting too much for my old heart."

"There's a newspaper article from the local paper, dated two years ago. Shall I read it?"

Everyone said "Yes!" at the same time, which made Quinn laugh. He sat forward in his seat, forearms on his knees, just as interested as the seniors.

"I had the pleasure of speaking with Mrs. Virginia Fortin about her life and times growing up near Amherst, and helping with her parents' business, Virginia's Cabins. Her mother died when she was fourteen and her younger brother was barely four, and she spent her early years building the business with her father and looking after her brother.

Throughout her life, Mrs. Fortin had been an avid flutist, and one summer day, a group of vacationers staying at the cabins heard her practicing in the forest. One of them was Alonsa Fabrice, the conductor of the Three Lakes Orchestra, who became Mrs. Fortin's guiding light. Through Ms. Fabrice's care, Virginia moved to Ottawa where she finished school and took flute lessons with a well-known teacher, winning many contests along the way. She joined the Ottawa Symphony Orchestra, which was then known as the Ottawa Civic Symphony, and performed with them until her marriage in 1970. Thankfully, she did not give up her love of the flute, as she often held impromptu performances at the cabins for customers.

Mrs. Fortin and her husband moved into one of the cabins at Virginia's Cabins while her husband helped her father and brother build two more cabins to expand the business. Upon the birth of the first of four children, the Fortins moved to a home of their own, closer to schools.

Mrs. Fortin is still an accomplished flutist and with little encouragement brought out her instrument and played a delightful rendition of Living in the Past by Jethro Tull (which quite surprised this reporter).

Her children have all moved away, and her brother still maintains the well-known and much-loved vacation spot of Virginia's Cabins, though there is talk of him selling the family business because of health reasons. Having enjoyed summers there myself as a youngster, I know many people hope the cabins will be there for future generations for many years to come."

Ellie finished reading the article and sat back in her chair. Everyone seemed to be lost in thought, considering everything they had just heard.

"So," Norma said slowly, "she was alive at least two years ago, and she lives in the area."

"I'm sure everyone around knows who she is and where we can find her," Shirley said.

"Except the Wagners!" Norma said.

"Ellie, what about trying 4-1-1?" Phil asked, sliding into the tried-and-true method that had helped them solve mysteries in the past. "You never know. She might have a landline. Some of us older folk still do."

"Wouldn't hurt," Ellie agreed, turning back to her computer. "Virginia Fortin, and let's enter Quebec as a whole to broaden the search."

Ruth leaned over and looked at the screen. "That's a lot."

"Easy to narrow down though," Ellie said as she skimmed through the listings. "Here! Virginia Fortin, 32 Elmer Road, Amherst. Do you want her phone number?"

Norma held up a hand. "No. I think I'd prefer to drop by."

"Oh." Jeremy shook his head. "That's not a good idea, Norma. It's never polite to do that."

"Maybe not," Norma said, chin raised as if daring anyone to say a word. "But I'd feel better simply driving up and knocking on the door. If it's not her, then it's not her. I—I wouldn't know what to say on the phone."

"I'm betting it's her," Ellie said.

Norma stood up in a rush and grabbed the back of her chair. "If you don't mind, I'd like to handle it this way."

"It's your choice," Ellie said, worried by how upset her aunt was becoming.

Phil went to his room and returned with a folded map of the area, which he spread out on the table. "Let's see where it is, then."

Quinn pulled out his phone and showed it to Phil. "We can do it with an app."

"No thanks," Phil said, lowering his face close to the map to read the names of places. "I like to do it the old way."

"Were you a Boy Scout, by any chance?" Shirley asked him.

"Why do you ask?"

"Because you're always prepared!"

Phil put a finger to the map and located where they were at the cabins. "What's the street name?"

Ellie checked her notes. "32 Elmer Road."

Phil shifted the map sideways to read the list of streets on the side panel, and noted the coordinates from the map. He turned it right side up, drew one hand down from the top and the other hand from the side in line with the coordinates, until they intersected at Elmer Road.

"Here it is!" He kept his finger on the spot and let Quinn look at the map. Phil put another finger on where the cabins were and left his finger on Elmer Road.

"That shouldn't take more than half an hour," Quinn said. "Is this out of the way of where you wanted to go next, Ellie?"

Ellie came to stand beside him and looked at Phil's fingers, still glued to their spots. She smiled. "Not by much, and it's a lovely drive along there."

"You said there was a surprise destination on the trip home, didn't you?" Jeremy asked, giving Quinn a fleeting glance.

"And a surprise it shall remain!"

Chapter Seventeen

Shirley and Ruth pulled out the last of the sandwiches and set them on the table. Ellie emptied a few bags of chips into bowls and placed them within easy reach of everyone.

When they were all seated, Norma spoke. "Thank you all for coming along with me on this..."

"Adventure?" Phil suggested, before taking a bite of his sandwich.

"It *is* an adventure, isn't it?" Norma said, leaving her food untouched. "I never thought anything would still be here, to be honest."

"I'm just glad we managed to find it in the dark," Jeremy said, helping himself to a handful of chips, and putting another handful on Ruth's plate.

"And I had a nightmare about Mr. Wagner shooting us," Shirley said. She shivered as if reliving it.

"Well, we'll be gone before you know it, and you'll never see him again," Ruth said, devouring her small pile of chips.

"I'll agree that this has been quite the experience," Jeremy said. "Even with the dip in the lake."

"Ha!" Ruth put her hand over her mouth. "If it hadn't been so cold, we could have gone swimming in those life jackets."

"And I'm glad you're both fine this morning," Ellie said. "I was worried."

"I've really enjoyed this place," Quinn said. "It's a great location, and the cabin is in good shape for being so old. I wonder how much they bought it for."

"Probably an arm and a leg," Norma said.

"Interesting tidbit," Ellie said. "I was looking at some addresses where my great-grandfather lived in London over the years, and there was a five room house the family once owned that is now on the market with a value worth close to six million pounds."

"What's that in Canadian dollars?" Jeremy asked.

"Around ten million, give or take," Ellie said. "But it is in Belgravia, which is a posh part of town these days. Lots of embassies and high commissions in the area. Quite different from when my great-grandfather lived there as a taxi driver! Oh, and it's down the road from the backside of Buckingham Palace, where the gardens are!"

"I'm going to search for my ancestors' old homes when we get back," Phil said. "Google maps is amazing. You can even see the actual building."

"I've also noted," said Ellie, "that my family moved around a lot. I made a list of all the addresses I could gather from census returns, birth documents, marriage certificates, death records, even school records. I printed out a map of London and put pins in every location where they lived. As my great-grandfather moved up in the world, he owned his own fleet of taxis, and moved his family into better areas. He wasn't rich, but he was comfortable."

"That's a great idea," Quinn said. "It might be interesting to find out where my family lived through their years in Scotland."

"I'll make a genealogist out of you, if you're not careful!" Ellie laughed.

"It's fascinating, actually." Quinn collected all the lunch wrappers, tossed them in the garbage, and wiped down the counters in the kitchen.

"I've lived in about six different places over my life," Phil said. "I'll do that for my memoir."

Shirley leaned into him and whispered, "I see you like the term as much as I do!"

Phil grinned at her and whispered back, "It *does* sound more dramatic than just writing our own personal histories."

"So," Ellie concluded, standing up and checking her watch. "It's time to pack and make sure nothing's been left anywhere. A final tour, checking under the beds and such, and then we'll head out to meet Virginia."

Everyone disappeared into their rooms. Beds were tided and suitcases packed.

"I don't think this belongs to me." Phil held up a red bra and looked from Norma to Shirley.

"Mine." Norma grabbed it from his hand and jammed it down into her suitcase, her face turning almost as bright red as her unmentionable had been.

"Don't forget to look everywhere," Ellie called from the living room.

"But I can't get down on my knees!" Phil complained.

"Fine, I'll do it." Norma got down on the ground and took a cursory check under the beds. "Just a herd of dust bunnies," she said before standing up.

Ruth and Jeremy had their room tidy and were the first back in the living room. They plopped down on the couch and waited. "Oh, darn!" Ruth scrambled up and headed for the bathroom. "Don't forget your toothbrushes," she called out. "And whoever's teeth are in a glass, come and get them."

Silence filled the cabin as the seniors looked at each other. Smiles appeared as they realized none of them had false teeth and Ruth was pulling their leg. But toothbrushes were retrieved and packed away.

When the bags were all by the front door, Ellie ran through the rooms for one last look. She came back from the bunkbed room with a single sock held up.

"Who does this belong to?"

Shirley raised her hand. "Mine! Where did you find it?"

"Between the bed and the wall." Ellie handed it to her. "The bigger question is, how did it get there?"

"It must have come off while I was sleeping," Shirley said. "My feet get cold at night."

"And you didn't miss it?" Phil asked.

Shirley shrugged.

Quinn carried the bags to the van and stowed them in the back.

"Wait," Ruth said before they followed him out. "Has everyone had a last trip to the loo? We don't know how long we'll be on the road."

Almost as one, they sighed and stood in line outside the bathroom.

Ten minutes later, the keys to the cabin were on the table, and the door was closed firmly behind them.

"One last group picture!" Ruth pulled her camera from her bag. "Everyone, please stand in front of the cabin. We can't all fit on the balcony."

"Here," Quinn reached for the camera. "You need to be in this picture."

Ruth bustled about, positioning Shirley and Phil together, Norma and Ellie, before taking her spot with Jeremy, their arms wrapped around each other.

"Say butter tarts!" Quinn called to them as he made sure everyone was in the shot and focused.

"Butter tarts!"

***

Quinn helped everyone into the van, then climbed into the driver's seat. They drove towards the office and Quinn honked the horn at Otto, who was struggling to move a picnic table. "Damn," Quinn said, stopping the van. "Sorry, folks, won't take long."

He hopped out and went over to Otto. "Where do you want this?"

Otto seemed ready to refuse the help, then noticed the faces in the van watching them, and changed his mind. "I need to move it in front of the second cabin, please."

They each took an end and crab walked the table down the road to the spot Otto had chosen. With a couple of placement adjustments, Otto finally nodded his approval, then held out his hand to Quinn. "Thank you. You've probably saved my back."

Quinn took Otto's hand and gave it a shake. "My pleasure. This is a great place here, Otto. I wish you the best with it."

They walked back to the office, not paying attention to the gawking seniors in the van. Quinn returned to his seat and tooted the horn goodbye before heading down the long driveway to the road.

"That was kind," Norma said from the back.

"Never hurts to help someone out," Quinn said, though he caught Ellie's grin. "Phil, you've got the coordinates?"

Phil pulled the map from the top clasp of his bag and settled it on his lap. He had folded in such a way that their exact destination was laid out from start to finish. "Roger that."

As they reached the end of the gravel road, Quinn looked back at Phil. "Left or right?"

Phil studied the map and angled it towards the window to see it better. "Left. The road should take us into the town where Virginia lives. It'll take about half an hour and there's lots of winding roads and hills."

"This could get boring," Shirley mumbled.

"Or we could play Never Have I Ever," Norma suggested from her seat beside Shirley.

Ellie swivelled around to gawk at her aunt. "When did you play Never Have I Ever?"

"My gosh, Ellie." Norma tossed her head. "Do you think we didn't play these types of games when we were young? That your age group invented everything? I could tell you stories."

"Please do," Jeremy said, sending her an impish grin.

"And how do you play this game?" Quinn asked, slowing down for a rabbit crossing the road.

"Quinn, have you never played it?" Norma asked in surprise.

"Afraid not." He caught her eye in the review mirror and watched Norma's left eyebrow spike.

"Don't we need booze for this game?" Shirley asked.

"What?" Quinn asked, startled by the comment.

"It wouldn't be smart to turn up at Virginia's door all sauced to the gills," Ruth said. "Can you imagine what she'd think of us?"

"Probably that we're having a grand old time," Jeremy said. He shifted in his seat to give Ruth more room, but she simply moved closer. He kissed her on the forehead and took her hand in his.

"So, we'll play the boring version," Norma said. "Are you listening, Quinn?"

"Yes, ma'am."

"We'll all start by holding up both hands, fingers out." She watched as everyone followed her instructions, except Quinn.

"How do I play?" Quinn asked. "I can drive with one hand, but these roads are tricky."

"Then remember it in your head," Ruth told him.

"I'm going to start," Norma said. "I'll say a statement, such as, never have I ever gone skinny dipping. You want to say something that you think other people may have done, but one that you have not. Now, if any of you *have* done the thing that anyone says they've never done, like skinny dipping, you put one finger down. Next person says something they've never done, and so on until there's only one person with a finger up. Any questions?"

"Got it," said Ruth.

"Sounds fun," Phil said.

"This is going to be a disaster," Ellie mumbled.

"I heard that," Norma called from the back. "Which means you go first. So, Ellie, what have you never done?"

"So, to clarify," Ellie said, "I want to say something that I think you've done so you lower a finger, but not something I've done."

"Correct." Norma nodded. "We're waiting."

"Give me a second." Ellie scrunched up her face, deep in thought. "Okay. I've got one. Never have I ever been on a plane."

Quinn turned to her. "Never?"

"And I doubt I ever will."

"We'll see about that." He threw her a quick grin, then returned his attention to the road. "That's one finger down for me."

Everyone except Ruth and Shirley lowered a finger.

"Quinn's turn," Jeremy said.

"Here's a good one" Quinn looked at them all in the review mirror to find everyone's eyes focused on him. "Never have I ever shot a gun."

They all looked at each other, hands held out and fingers dropped. First Phil, then Jeremy, Shirley, and finally Norma.

"Aunt Norma!" Ellie's eyes were wide. "When did you ever shoot a gun? I can understand the guys, and even Shirley working on the farm all those years, but you?"

Norma's lips pursed together, and she gave her niece a squinty stare. "There's a lot you don't know about me, my dear. Your uncle gave me a pistol on our first anniversary."

"How romantic." Shirley rolled her eyes.

"You'll never know *how* romantic that was," Norma said. "I went to the pistol range and won ribbons at shooting contests."

"Why haven't I ever seen them?" Ellie asked.

"It's not something I like to advertise. My turn." Norma closed her eyes in concentration and smiled mischievously. "Never have I ever baked a turkey dinner. That was my husband's forte."

"Oh, that's not fair!" Ruth laughed as she lowered her finger.

But what surprised them all was that everyone except Shirley put a finger down, including Quinn.

"Really?" Ellie asked him. "You cooked a turkey dinner?"

"My Gran loved them, but at the end of her life, it was too much for her."

"You get to keep a finger, Shirley." Ruth grinned at her sister. "But I am impressed by you men. Well done!"

"You'd be surprised at all the things we can do," Phil said. "I'm next. Never have I ever driven a tractor."

"That's a good one," Shirley said as she lowered a finger. "But I have. So have you, Ruth, even though it was just that once."

Ruth lowered a finger in acknowledgement. "I was so scared!"

"That's one I haven't done," Jeremy said.

Ellie's finger was still up, but she looked back to catch Norma lowering one of hers. "Aunt Norma! When did you drive a tractor? You're making that up."

"Why would I want to lower a finger if I didn't have to?" Norma shook her head at the ridiculousness of the comment. "You know how much I love to win."

But Ellie noticed her aunt hadn't answered her question.

"My turn," Ruth said. "Let's see. Never have I ever been married."

Quinn caught Jeremy's eye in the mirror and stifled a quick grin. With any luck that "never" would be remedied soon.

"Well," Jeremy said, "that leaves Ruthie and Shirley out."

"And me," Quinn said.

"Never married?" Norma asked quietly. "Seems a shame. You'd make a good catch."

"Thank you, Norma." Quinn turned red. "Are you offering?"

"Gosh, no!" She let out a braying hoot. "You'd never keep up with me!"

As the laughter died down, Shirley put her hand in the air. "Looks like it's now a tie between Quinn, Ellie, and myself."

"Then I'll go next," Jeremy said. "Never have I ever gotten drunk."

"Oh, for pity's sake!" Norma said as she closed the fingers of one hand and lowered it to her lap.

Phil, Quinn and Ruth also lowered a finger.

"When did you get drunk?" Jeremy asked Ruth.

"Well, it was a long time ago," she mumbled. He leaned his head to hers and they stayed there for a minute, as if he knew it had something to do with the time they were torn apart.

"Right," Shirley said loudly. "My turn. It would appear that Ellie and I are tied, so let's see how this one goes. Never have I ever been in a physical fight."

The group held their breath, not knowing what Ellie's answer would be. But her finger remained up. She was still in the game. But all the men and Norma lowered another finger, Norma and Phil having to go to their other hand.

"I hate to break this up," Phil said, scanning the map in his lap, "but we're almost there."

"Shall we call it a tie, Shirley?" Ellie asked.

Shirley took a breath, her competitive nature on full view. "Sure, why not. It was fun."

"But you'd rather win," Ruth said, stealing a glance back at her sister.

"Who wouldn't?" Shirley agreed.

"I'm with you there, Shirley," Norma said.

Chapter Eighteen

"We're looking for Elm Street," Phil said, rechecking the map on his lap. "It'll be to the left."

Ellie paid attention to the street signs as they passed. "Whoa!" She turned in her seat as they drove by a road. "That was it. The sign was hidden behind some bushes."

"I can't see any place to reverse up ahead. I'll do a three-point turn," Quinn said. "No cars either way?" Even though he brought the group into the maneuver, he was the one responsible for everyone staying safe.

"Are you sure you can do this?" Shirley asked, her eyes glued to the windows, her head swivelling back and forth from the road behind to the road ahead.

Quinn focused on backing up and turning. "No worries." The van was large, and it took a couple more steps than normal.

"Nice driving," Norma said. "Big vehicles are murder to turn around quickly."

Once again, Ellie threw her aunt a curious stare. "You've driven big vehicles?"

Norma shrugged and smiled. "You know, your uncle had one, and I may have had to drive it a few times."

"I've never seen you drive anything except your little Mini Cooper," Ellie said.

"Which is a great car for me at this period of my life. Very efficient."

"But you can't drive it in the winter," Phil said. "I mean, some people consider that a sports car, and these snowy roads would kill it."

"It manages, but I don't like to drive *any* car during the winter, so I put it away," Norma said. "Are we here?"

Everyone had been so engrossed in the idea of tiny Norma driving a big truck that they had missed the fact that they had stopped. A long curving driveway led up to a large country style home, with a wrap-around balcony and tall trees along the sides and in the back. A small raised garden occupied the front lawn, the only place that had full sunshine.

And planted at the foot of the driveway was a For Sale sign.

"This is it," Phil said, looking from the street civic number to the paper in his hands. "33 Elm."

"It's for sale," Shirley said. "She might not even be here!"

"What do you want to do?" Ellie asked Norma.

"Well." Norma had put little thought into this part of the adventure.

"We really should have called her first," Ruth said. "All these people turning up on her doorstep will be quite a shock."

"Maybe it's not her," Phil said.

"The facts would say otherwise." Norma stared at the house, as if that would somehow reveal the truth.

"But we should do something soon," Quinn said, "because parking here is sure to raise eyebrows and possibly make her nervous."

"Fine," Norma said, tossing her hands in the air. "I'll go to the door and find out if this is Virginia. If she even opens up to a stranger!"

Quinn parked near the front and jumped out to pull the sliding door open for Norma. He helped her to the ground. "Do you want me to come with you?"

Norma squeezed his hand and plastered a smile on her face. "I'm nervous, but I have to do this myself."

He stood by and watched her trudge up the steps to the porch. She hesitated before ringing the bell and turned to give him a quick nod. No one came, so she rang the bell again. Nothing.

Norma's shoulders slumped as she left the porch.

"Hello, hello!" A little lady with designer glasses barreled around the side of the house. "I'm sorry, but you have to make an appointment with the agent to view the house." She came to an abrupt stop when she saw Norma. It was as if time had slipped away for both of them. Tentative smiles crossed their faces before Virginia held out her arms and squealed, "Norma! You haven't changed a bit!"

Norma hesitated for a second before being pulled into Virginia's hug. And it was a powerful hug. Virginia smelled liked sunshine and flowers. When she stepped back, she kept her hands on Norma's arms while they both stared at each other.

"You look the same," Virginia said in an awed whisper. "How do you do it?"

Norma took another step back, and Virginia's hands slid down to grasp Norma's. "My gosh, Virginia," Norma was shocked. "You look the same too! Though I love the new glasses."

Virginia touched the rim of her wire-frame glasses and winked. "This was the best purchase I've ever made. Those huge ones I wore got so heavy!"

"And you kept your long hair." Norma touched the curls that reached Virginia's shoulders in silky grey waves.

Virginia cocked her head and searched past Norma to the street. "And who is that gorgeous man leaning against the van?" she asked in a lowered voice. "Is he yours?"

"Oh, Virginia!" Norma laughed. "He's a good friend, and my niece's beau. But I have so much to tell you. I'm here with my seniors genealogy group and I was wondering if we could..."

Before Norma could finish, Virginia was making a beeline for the van. "Come in, come in! Any friend of Norma's is a friend of mine! Welcome to my home."

Quinn grinned back at Norma, who hadn't moved from the bottom of the stairs, and helped everyone out of the van. They all shook hands with Virginia and introduced themselves. When it was Ellie's turn, Virginia took one look at her and then turned to Norma.

"She looks the spitting image of you when you were young!" Virginia grabbed Ellie and pulled her in for a big hug. Virginia was a hugger.

"Thank you," Ellie said, staggering a bit when Virginia finally released her.

"Come in, all of you." Virginia headed back to the house and held the door open for them all to enter. "The kitchen is probably best, as it's got more room. Straight down the hall to the end and grab a seat."

As they all made their way through the house, Ellie stopped Norma before they reached the kitchen. "How do you want to handle this?"

"She's such a sweetie," Norma said. "I don't know if this will hurt her or not."

"I doubt it," said Quinn, who had stopped behind them. "I think she'll be tickled. What a story to tell. Here." He handed Norma the bag of jewelry she'd left on her seat.

They met the others in the kitchen, all seated at an enormous table. Virginia was at the stove putting two kettles on to boil.

"Tea is all I have, I'm afraid," Virginia said as she bustled around the room, pulling down cups and setting milk, sugar, and spoons on the table. "Never was a coffee drinker, and neither was my husband."

"You married?" Norma asked, sliding onto a chair beside Ellie and resting the bag on her lap. She knew the answer to the question, but needed a minute to settle her nerves. She glanced around the room, not having glimpsed any other part of the house as they'd hurried down the hall moments before. The kitchen was large, a gas stove lined the far wall, with prep counters down the two adjacent walls. One held a sink, the other a refrigerator, and an island separated it all from the table where they now sat.

"I did indeed," Virginia said. "And the family continues to grow." She waved a hand at the refrigerator door, which was covered in pictures of children of all ages.

"Are those all yours?" Ruth asked in astonishment.

"Four children and eight grandchildren," Virginia said as she put the cups on the table. "Christmas around here has gotten to be quite overwhelming, though the family all pitch in now. Truth be told, this is the only house that will hold us all! As much as I love it here, it's too big and the kids have all agreed I should sell and get something smaller."

"And your husband?" Norma asked, fearing the answer as she had noticed nothing that would show Virginia had someone living with her.

"Oh, poor Simon." Virginia shook her head and sighed. "Died about fifteen years ago, heart attack."

"Same for my husband," Norma said quietly. "I'm sorry."

"Right back at ya," Virginia said. "I'm not being glib about it, but that's life. And he did like his hamburgers, no matter what anyone told him."

Quinn hadn't sat down, but watched the older woman getting the tea together. When Virginia took the kettles from the stove, he strode in and took them from her. "Just tell me where to put them."

Virginia grinned. "Oh, it is good to have a man about the place!" She put some rubber mats on the table and motioned for him to put them down. "Help yourselves, everyone. It's only tea bags, but I hope that's okay."

"You don't have to go to this trouble, Virginia," Norma said. "It's very rude of me to drop by like this, unannounced and all."

"You have no idea how many times I've thought about you over the years, Norma," Virginia said before jumping up and taking a full bag of Oreo cookies from the cupboard and emptying them onto a plate. She placed it in the middle and took one before resuming her seat.

"You'll never guess where we spent last night," Shirley said to her.

Virginia looked confused and then let out a laugh. "Not Virginia's Cabins?"

"It's a marvellous place," Jeremy said. "The fishing isn't too good right now, but I understand how people would want to stay there for a week or more."

"Oh, five days was the longest we let anyone stay," Virginia said. "We had so many complaints from people who couldn't reserve a cabin that we had to limit it. And then we built another cabin, so that helped too. So, what do you think of the new owners?"

"Well." Norma struggled to come up with something nice to say. "I think they're going to make a few changes. They want to move in above the office and rent out their cabin."

"That's a good idea," Virginia nodded. "It wasn't big enough for our family to do that, but I can see the sense."

"I cannot imagine how he'll make a success out of this," Shirley burst out. "He's not a people person, at all!"

"Maybe we got him on an off day," Ellie suggested, always one to spot the good in people.

"My brother told me about them when we sold," Virginia said. "It was getting too much for him and his family to deal with and it was time. Turned out well."

"We were talking about how things go up in value over the years," Phil said, taking a second Oreo and twisting it apart before scraping the white insides out with his teeth. He froze like a deer in the headlights when he saw they were all staring at him. "What? I love eating them like this."

"I think we won't talk about property valuations and such, Phil," Ruth said, before twisting her own cookie open and following Phil's lead. "It's a personal thing."

Chapter Nineteen

"Do you remember playing hide and seek at night, Norma?" Virginia asked, stirring her tea, the spoon clinking against the side. "And how dark it got?"

"I loved it." Norma smiled. "I'm not sure if it was because there were no lights around at all, but I could see really well."

"Not me!"

"I recall a rather nasty head bump you got. Your mother was furious at us."

"That was right before the jewelry theft," Virginia said, as if it had happened to someone else and she was simply retelling a story told to her.

The group went so quiet and still that Virginia knew something was up. She looked from one to the other. "What?"

"So," Norma said. She touched the bag in her lap and took a deep breath. "This isn't just a hi, how are you kind of visit."

"No, I figured as much," Virginia said. She set her teacup down and gave Norma her full attention. "Why did you really go back to the cabins?"

"Do you remember the last time my family vacationed there?"

"Vividly." Virginia nodded. "I never knew why you didn't come back, and I was very distraught. I thought, as all children did, that it was something I had done."

"Oh, gosh no!" Norma shook her head. "You never did anything wrong, Virginia. You were the sweetest kid."

The seniors remained quiet, watching the interplay between the old friends.

"You were like an idol to me, Norma. You always let me hang around when you went on your adventures. You explained nature to me, why animals behaved certain ways, how different flowers grew where they did."

"I loved how curious you were."

"I had so many things I wanted to do in life, but I loved my flute!"

"And I hear you turned that into something special."

"Lived my dream! I played in the Ottawa Symphonic Orchestra for a few years before I got pregnant with my first. It was the best time of my life. Do you remember telling me you were going to be a spy? Did that ever happen?"

Norma smiled, but refused to meet everyone's surprised eyes. "So, the reason we stayed at the cabins yesterday was because I wanted to find something I had buried there the day before we left."

Virginia looked confused. "I don't understand."

Norma slowly pulled the bag from her lap and placed it on the table. She pushed it towards Virginia. "I believe these belong to you."

Virginia reached for the bag but caught Norma's gaze. "You look so sad, Norma. What's going on?" She opened it and peeked inside, then gasped.

Norma closed her eyes. There was no going back now. She heard the pieces of jewelry clink to the table and the slight moan coming from Virginia.

"Did you steal them?" Virginia said, her voice a mix of hush and dread.

"No!" Norma said. "I hid them so they'd never be lost. But I messed that up."

A string of pearls slipped through Virginia's fingers, and a smile played across her lips. "These were my mom's favorite. She used to let me wear them for dress up, but only when she was around. And this." She picked up a glittering broach in the shape of a butterfly. "This belonged to my mom's great-grandmother. I never knew her name."

All heads perked up and swiveled to Ellie. She quickly shook her head no, as if to say this was not the time or place to talk about genealogy.

"So, how did you get them?" Virginia finally looked Norma in the eye. Any hint of anger or blame vanished. Instead, she had a sheen of unshed tears and a crooked smile of happiness.

Norma leaned on the table and held out her hands, waiting for Virginia to take hold. When their fingers entwined, Norma began her story.

"Do you remember my Uncle Tommy?"

"I think so." Virginia appeared to search her memory. "Didn't he stay in the spill over cabin that last night before you left?"

"Yes, he did. Uncle Tommy had a disease called kleptomania."

"Oh, goodness." Virginia disengaged their hands and sat back. "Oh, the poor man. He was so sweet. He helped me put the chain on my bike that day. Actually, he taught me how to do it!"

"That's the terrible thing," Norma agreed. "He *was* sweet, but he stole things, a lot of things. He never did it on purpose, or with a plan, or sold the goods, or anything. But he got caught a few times."

"Did he ever go to jail?" Jeremy asked from the end of the table.

"No," Norma said. "But another conviction would send him right inside, mental illness or not."

The room became quiet except for Phil slurping his tea. Quinn fidgeted in his seat, and Ruth sighed.

"So, on the day of the games, while the games were actually happening, Uncle Tommy snuck into your cabin and came out with something in his hands. He dashed around the back of the rental cabins until he got to his and ran inside. A few minutes later he left and headed down to the beach to join the games."

"You weren't at the games that day," Virginia said. "Stomach bug."

"You remember that?"

"You threw up on the dock. I think we all remember that!"

"Good thing too, because I saw what Uncle Tommy did. And when he headed to the beach, I ran inside and searched for whatever he'd taken from your cabin. And I found them."

"My gosh. Why didn't you just return them?"

"Because Uncle Tommy would have gone to jail."

"But my parents wouldn't have done anything if they got it all back," Virginia assured her. "You have no idea what happened after that. My mother wanted to call the police right away, but my dad said he'd handle it."

"Virginia," Norma said urgently. "I was ten years old. I wasn't thinking like an adult. In my mind, it was black and white. There was only jail for Uncle Tommy, and I couldn't let that happen."

"So, what did you do with everything?"

"I buried it."

"What?" Virginia looked flabbergasted. "How did you do that?"

"While everyone was at the games, I got a garden shovel and found a spot under a tree root, beside a rock, and I dug and dug. There was already a small hole underneath, and I pushed the jewelry into it. It was in a plastic bag, so I thought it would be safe."

"Well, it's been safe for over sixty years!" Phil said.

"I thought I'd come back and dig it up another year and present it like a great finding."

"But you never came back," Virginia said softly.

"No, we didn't," Norma said. "And that was my fault. I never wanted the possibility of Uncle Tommy returning there. He came with us a lot over the years, but that was the first time I saw what he could do. It scared me. I made all sorts of excuses not to go back to Virginia's Cabins, and my parents didn't seem to mind. We stopped going camping after that."

"You must have hated that," Virginia said.

"You have no idea!"

"Well, after you all left the next day, the police came," Virginia said. "They searched all the cabins, but found nothing."

"Did they ever suspect it was us?" Norma asked, dreading the answer.

"Never," Virginia said. "It was written off as someone passing through, stealing while everyone was at the games."

"In a way, that's exactly what happened," Norma said. "I'm so sorry, Virginia. Sorry for not having the strength or courage to come back before now."

Virginia looked at the array of jewelry in front of her and picked up a delicate diamond ring. "My grandson is getting engaged, and the poor boy has been stressing about what kind of ring to get. I think this would be perfect!"

But Jeremy's eyes were on a smaller cameo ring buried under the jumble of jewelry.

Chapter Twenty

"So, tell me about this group you all belong to," Virginia said as everyone finished their tea. She appeared to enjoy their company and didn't want them to go. "You all seem like such a tight-knit bunch."

"Well," Norma said. "My niece has been teaching us how to write our life stories."

"Memoirs, Norma," Shirley reminded, putting her empty teacup on the table. "We are a little more high-brow than just writing our life stories."

"Well, maybe you are," Ruth said to her sister, "but the rest of us quite like it being about our life stories. It sounds more encompassing."

"Seems complicated," Virginia said.

Ellie jumped in. "Not at all. Every week we have a topic, such as finding our birth certificate, or drawing a floor plan for the homes we've lived in."

"That was one of my favorites," Jeremy said.

"And then we write about the topics, first in bullet points, things we remember, things we're not sure of and need to check. After that we expand, fill it in with color, and some mentions of other people who were there, or the emotions we felt at the moment."

"My goodness," Virginia said. "I can only imagine my kids reading about what I was like before they were born!"

"Oh, don't worry," Norma said. "You don't have to share it. You can burn it if you like, or leave it for the family to read when you're dead."

"And what are *you* going to do?" Virginia asked Norma. "I still don't know if you have secrets to hide!"

Once again, Ellie turned a startled face to her aunt. Ellie wasn't sure if the comment was in jest, but Norma didn't respond.

"I'm leaving my story to my son and grandkids," Jeremy said. "But there are a few things I probably won't write about. Better let some things rest."

The seniors knew he was talking about his time in Europe during World War II.

"Well, it sounds absolutely top-notch fun," Virginia said. "How do I join?"

Ellie thought about it, but it was Phil who answered the question. "Could we hook her up with us through Zoom? Like a conference call thingy?"

"Can I get back to you on that, Virginia?" Ellie asked. "Could you manage that on the computer yourself?"

"Are you kidding?" Norma laughed. "You only needed to show Virginia something once and she got it down. Amazing ability. Which is why she's such an excellent flute player."

Virginia turned pink with Norma's praise before focusing on Ellie. "Did I hear right? You're a genealogist?"

"Yes," Ellie said. "I have many clients, and I sometimes do all the actual research, but I like to set out a plan for them so they can do the detective work themselves. Most people enjoy the actual finding of ancestors."

Virginia jumped up abruptly and left the room, returning seconds later with a gold-framed picture. She handed it to Ellie. "Can you help me find her?"

"Who is she?" Ruth asked.

"She was the owner of the diamond ring." Virginia held it up for all to see. "And I'd like to learn more about her. How would you go about setting out a plan? I'll pay you, of course."

"Oh, lord." Quinn groaned from his seat at the end of the table. "Don't get her started!" After receiving a well-aimed kick in the shin from Ellie, he took another cookie and sat back, trying to hide a grin while he watched Ellie in her element.

"This is very basic, and I'd give you a much more detailed search plan if we were doing it for real." Ellie threw Quinn a quick smile. "I always start with one question. What do you want to find out? Here, you want to find out about this woman. I would hope you could provide a bit of information, besides her name, of course. Like, where did she live? How are you descended from her, meaning what's the line from her to you? Then you'd work backwards. So, from your parents, who were *their* parents? You'd try to find them in census returns. With that information, you might find their parents and so on, until you get to this woman. Of course, there are other records I'd recommend you searching, not just census returns, so you have a better chance of finding something. Do you have any information about her at all?"

"She was my great-grandmother on my father's side and her first name was Hattie," Virginia said. "And that's all I know about her. I want to find out who her people were. I'm pretty sure she came from England, but her husband was born here and they married here. And where would I look for the census returns?"

Norma held up a hand to stop any more questions. "Ellie will make up a plan for you, with all the resources you'll need to start a search. And she'll be available for help, if you need it."

"That's a bit high handed," Shirley said. "Offering Ellie's services like that."

"Shirley." Ellie shook her head. "Don't you know me by now? That's exactly what I'm going to do! And I'm not charging you a penny, Virginia. Any friend of my Aunt Norma's is a friend of mine."

Quinn took a quick glance at his watch and caught Ellie's eye, raising an eyebrow in question.

Ellie stood up. "And now, unfortunately, we have to leave. We have one more stop on our trip, and I think everyone is getting tired."

As they all got up, Ellie quickly and efficiently cleared the table while final goodbyes were being said.

"Oh, wait!" Virginia disappeared into the living room and returned with another picture frame. She held this one to her chest and stood before Norma.

"Ready?" With a flourish, she turned it around to reveal two young girls standing in front of a cabin at Virginia's Cabins. One girl had pigtails, huge glasses, carried a flute, and was staring at the other girl with outright admiration. The other girl had a hand on her hips, a fishing rod at her feet, and a fish in the other hand.

Norma reached for the picture. "Oh, Virginia, how did you get this?"

"Your mom wasn't the only one who loved to take photographs! My mom snapped pictures of everyone, and it cost a fortune to get them developed. But my dad loved how excited she got. She always took a picture of each family or group as they were leaving. Most of them ended up on the wall behind the reception desk. But Mom took this picture right in the middle of your stay. She'd never seen a girl catch a fish before."

"I wanted to teach you to fish," Norma said before looking at her friend. "But you hated to touch the worms and remove the fish from the hooks."

"I can relate," Phil said sheepishly.

Virginia took the picture from Norma and started fiddling with the back. She pulled the cover off and removed a second copy from inside before putting the frame back together. "Here." She handed it to Norma. "I always thought I'd find you one day, so I've kept a copy. This picture captured how much you meant to me when we were growing up. You were always so kind."

Norma threw her arms around her friend and hugged her close. "You've got to come and visit me, Virginia. Stay for a while."

"I'd be delighted to," Virginia answered, her voice muffled in Norma's hair.

They exchanged phone numbers, gave more hugs, and were finally out the front door.

"Wait!" Ruth hollered to them, stopping everyone in their tracks. "I need a picture of all of us. Quinn, could you..."

But he was already at the van, taking her camera from her bag. "I'll take the picture. You guys all gather around. Virginia, you better be in there too!"

"Your mom's not the only person who loves taking pictures!" Norma laughed, her arm tight around her friend's shoulders.

With a little moving and shuffling, they all found suitable positions, smiled for the camera, and said their last goodbyes.

"I have to use the facilities," Jeremy called out as seatbelts were being snapped closed. He jumped out and whispered to Virginia on the porch before they both disappeared inside.

"How long until our next stop?" Ruth asked Ellie.

"Half an hour. Does anyone else need to go?"

Everyone shook their heads no, and within minutes Jeremy strode out of the house and turned to give Virginia a hug. He hopped back into the van and gave Quinn a silly grin. "Ready to go, sir!"

As they drove down the driveway, Norma turned once more and waved at Virginia, who stood on the porch, picture frame in hand, waving back at her, a huge smile on her face.

***

"Gosh," Ruth said as she leaned into Jeremy. "This has been quite the trip."

"So, we have one more stop to make." Ellie turned in her seat to speak. "Is everyone up for it? It's on the way home and I promise you won't be disappointed."

"Can we nap until we get there?" Shirley asked from the back.

"Of course." Ellie laughed. "Or we can talk more genealogy."

Phil's hand went flying up. "Can we ask questions?"

"Sure thing, Phil. What's on your mind?" She gave Quinn a sweet smile and sat back to hear what Phil had to say.

"Hold on," Norma interrupted. "Let Shirley get settled. I think she's dozing."

"I'm good," Shirley said. "Just because my eyes are closed, it doesn't mean I'm not listening. What's up, Phil?"

Phil turned to Shirley and grinned when he saw she had indeed closed her eyes. Turning back to Ellie, he spoke in a lower voice so as not to disturb Shirley. She hadn't slept well, but then again, none of them had.

"I was wondering about records from other countries, and how do we go about searching them."

"Goodness," Ellie said, eyes open wide with surprise. "That's an entire week's worth of discussions right there. But you could use the big sites, like Ancestry, Family Search, and MyHeritage, to name a few. You can Google a country name and add the word genealogy research or records. There are a lot of free sites out there, and some for pay. I recently found a group in Newfoundland who were working together to transcribe and upload church records. So, there are tons of places. And don't forget joining genealogy societies in different locations where your ancestors lived. The genealogy community is extremely helpful. I had a woman in London track down a tombstone for me in Brompton Cemetery in London. She took the time to go there, took a picture of the tombstone, and send it to me."

"Not everything is on the internet though, is it?" Jeremy asked.

"Not by a long shot," Ellie said. "Sometimes it's fun to visit the actual places where our ancestors lived."

"I'll not be heading off to England anytime soon," Phil said.

"I get that," Ellie said. "But you can use Google maps to visit various places. Some homes don't exist anymore, but you can get an idea of what the neighbourhood might have been like."

"Where does your mother's family come from, Ellie?" Ruth asked. "I just realized that you don't mention her very much."

Ellie fell silent.

"Ellie's mother," Norma said, "was a wonderful woman. Her name was Lisa Purvis, and I never saw my brother so happy as when he was with her. She loved to give hugs and always had a smile on her face."

"It's sad to say, but to me, at that age, she was just my mom," Ellie said quietly. "You'd think by now I would have searched for her in every record I could find. And I've wanted to."

"What's stopped you?" Quinn asked, glancing at her.

"My dad."

"I don't understand," Ruth said, worry lines crossing her forehead.

"My mom was...fragile," Ellie said softly. "But she had a bond with my father you see only in movies. They were tight, and neither would let anything hurt the other. I remember asking her about her parents one time, if she had siblings, where she came from. I must have been about eight, and I didn't think there was anything different with my family until a class at school where we were talking about brothers and sisters. The teacher asked who had them and who didn't. I raised my hand for being an only child. I was the only one who raised their hand. It felt really strange. My friends all had brothers and sisters, but it never occurred to me that there might be a reason why I didn't."

"Oh, Ellie," Norma said. "Did they tell you?"

"They did." Ellie shifted into a more comfortable position and continued. "My mom almost died having me, and she had an operation so she couldn't have more children."

"Was that really necessary?" Shirley piped up from beside Norma, her eyes now open, her full attention focused on Ellie's sad face.

"Who knows," Ellie said. "But that's when I started asking questions. Lots of questions."

"And it upset her?" Jeremy asked.

"It did." Ellie nodded. "And that upset my dad. He told me not to ask questions again, ever, that there were some things in my mom's life she didn't want to relive. It scared me so much that I never *did* ask another question. I never wanted to cause her any pain."

"And you've never once wanted to learn about your mother and her family?" Phil asked in astonishment, not believing it for a minute.

"Oh, no, I have. Every day," Ellie said. "But I'm also worried about what I'll find, who I'll find, why it was so important for my mom to let it go and never bring it into our family. And I felt I needed to honor my dad's wishes."

"Oh, that's baloney!" Shirley said, shifting in her seat as if upset.

"It is," Ellie agreed. "And that's why I've written out a plan for myself to find her and her family."

It seemed as if everyone gasped together and then started talking all at once.

"Good for you!" Norma said.

"About time," Ruth mumbled.

"Are you sure you want to do this?" Phil asked.

Ellie held up a hand. "We all know I'm a put-my-head-in-the-sand type of gal for some things, but this was getting ridiculous. A genealogist who doesn't have her own family tree. It makes me feel like a fraud. But I've carried a lot around for the last few years and it's time to find the truth. I need to do this."

"You've carried a lot around since you were twelve," Norma muttered. "Don't do this if it might cause you anymore pain, Ellie. Losing your parents so young, and then your husband and daughter, you don't need more grief."

"But that's just it," Ellie said with a smile. "The truth can be painful, but it can also set you free."

"Have you got that stitched on a pillow somewhere?" Shirley asked before Norma nudged her in the ribs.

Chapter Twenty-One

Quinn pulled through the impressive gate house of the Fairmont Chateau Montebello and drove along the winding road. Bicyclists rode on the bike path beside them, and a little girl waved. They passed the huge log hotel structure and followed the signs to a guest parking lot next to a building that looked like an old wooden church.

"I know this place," Jeremy said. "Parc Omega is down the road, right? I took Sam when he was young. They have amazing animals there. But we could never afford to stay here!"

Quinn got out and pulled the van's doors open, offering his hand to help everyone exit. Ellie hopped down from her seat and stretched while they all gathered around.

"This is the surprise?" Shirley asked. "You're putting us up in luxury?" Her eyes scanned the immaculate grounds, the flower beds and groups of bushes, well maintained majestic trees and pathways.

"Not exactly," Ellie said. "While the Chateau itself is amazing, the history of this whole area is what I wanted to share with you. And there's a building I thought you might like to see, down the road a bit. I think we can walk there."

"Well, my legs need to move," Ruth said, taking Jeremy's arm and waiting for Ellie to lead the way. She missed the winks and nods between Jeremy, Ellie and Quinn, but Shirley caught it and was suddenly energized and eager to get to their destination. She knew what was to come.

"First of all," Ellie said, pointing back to the church-like building they had parked by. "This land is one of the seigneurial lands originally given to settlers. The Papineau family received this parcel, and they converted this building into the Family Museum. People used it for various purposes besides a museum, such as a gymnasium. Later, in 1935, they transformed it into a chapel."

"It's lovely," Norma said, stepping off the path to get a peek at a window on the side. "This is beautiful. I've always loved architecture."

"This entire section we're about to walk through is now owned by Parcs Canada," Ellie said as she continued down the road. "Oh, and the main log building? You saw how massive it is? Guess how long it took to build it?"

"At least a year," Quinn said.

"Four months," Ellie said with a grin. "It was a construction marvel."

"And this huge mansion?" Phil asked, stopping in the middle of the road to admire the large grey building, though this one was not built from logs.

"That is the Papineau Mansion where the family lived. They offer guided tours through it, but that's for another day."

"Can you smell that?" Jeremy asked. "Gosh, it smells like heaven in here. There are so many trees. Maybe because these old buildings make it feel like we're back in time, my mind is tricking me into thinking the air is cleaner!"

"Well, I hear the birds, that's for sure," Shirley said. "And kids having fun." Squeals of delight came from childish voices from the swimming pool's direction.

Ellie stopped a few feet down the road and motioned to a smaller building. "And this is the Granary, which held, well, grain. Don't quote me on this, as I'm not up on the complete history of the place, but..."

"You're giving us a free guided tour!" Norma said. "I'm in! Tell us what you know."

"What I specifically wanted to show you," Ellie said as they continued slowly past the Manoir and through the woods along the path, "was this." She stopped in front of an old metal fence at the entrance to what appeared to be a small chapel.

Pine trees surrounded it, and the round window above the wooden door caught the afternoon sun.

"This is perfect," Jeremy said in a whisper. His hand rummaged in his pocket and a look of panic crossed his face before his fingers latched onto what he was searching for. Just as he was about to drop to a knee, a couple came over to him, pushing their camera towards him.

"Could you take our picture please?" the young man said, his arm tight around his lady friend. "This is the most romantic place!"

The couple stood in front of the chapel, arms around each other, heads touching, smiles that could light up a room. Jeremy took a few pictures and handed the camera back, nodding at their many thank yous.

Once they had left, Jeremy gave Quinn and Ellie a quick nod. "Ruthie, isn't this the most beautiful place?"

"It truly is memorable, Jeremy." Ruth turned to Ellie. "Thank you dear, for this brief excursion. You know how much I love history, but for some reason I've never been here before."

Quinn and Ellie exchanged glances and tried to hide their grins. This was actually happening!

Ruth turned back to find Jeremy struggling to lower himself to the ground. When he was on one knee in front of her, he gently took her hand in his, pulled out the ring Virginia had graciously given him, and looked up at his first and deepest love.

"Oh, heavens!" Ruth gasped.

The others stood still, barely breathing at what they were witnessing. But Quinn had Ruth's camera, and snapped a lot of pictures.

A group of tourists walked towards them, boisterous and laughing. But when they noticed what was happening, they too stopped to watch, going quiet. An older couple behind them shared a glance and reached out their hands to one another.

"Ruthie," Jeremy said, a catch in his voice. "Ruthie, would you do me the most wonderful honour of being my wife?"

"Oh, Jeremy," Ruth pulled at him. "Get up, dear, your knee!"

Quinn hurried over and helped Jeremy up, then returned to Ellie's side, camera still poised and at the ready.

"You haven't answered," Jeremy said.

"Oh, of course I'll marry you!" Ruth said as the tears gathered. Jeremy put the ring on her finger and everyone cheered, including the tourists.

Complete strangers came up and congratulated them, asking if they could take pictures of the beaming couple. And all the while, Quinn captured every moment on camera as well.

"Hooray!" Shirley said, pulling Ruth and Jeremy into a big hug. "And you'll have to move in with us, Jeremy, because like I said, I'll be darned if I move into a retirement home!"

"I can't believe this!" Ruth giggled, holding out her hand to admire the delicate cameo ring.

"You don't mind that it's not a diamond?" Jeremy asked, a frown crossing his face.

"I never was one for jewelry." Ruth leaned into him and rested her head against his. "This is the most gorgeous ring I've ever seen. It's perfect." She sniffled.

Jeremy pulled back to look at her. "Are you crying?"

"Just happy tears." Ruth took the Kleenex Ellie passed to her. "Thank you, dear." She dabbed at her eyes and tucked the tissue up her sleeve.

"We have a lot of planning to do, Ruth," Shirley said from behind her. "My goodness, you'll need a dress!" Shirley gave her sister a quick squeeze, her excitement evident.

Ruth hugged her sister tight. "You'll have to help me with this, Shirley. I have no idea what to do."

"Are you having a big ceremony?" Phil asked. "And where are you going to hold it?"

"Oh, I don't think so," Ruth said, before turning to Jeremy. "Unless you want a big wedding."

"No," Jeremy said. "That's the last thing I want. Just family and good friends."

"Where *are* we going to hold it, and when? And what about food and..." Ruth's voice was rising, a tinge of panic creeping in.

"Perhaps Ellie can help you make a plan," Norma soothed, smiling at the joy coming from the engaged couple. "I hear she's very good at that."

"Would you, dear?" Ruth asked Ellie.

"With pleasure." Ellie pulled one of her ever-present notebooks out of her backpack and clicked her pen open. "Let's begin."

Chapter Twenty-Two

The senior group was already eating their snack when Ellie arrived for their scheduled meeting. All eyes turned to her and a hush came over them. It spooked her a bit.

Maggie waved at her from behind the counter. "Hey there! I'm very busy, catering a wedding. We'll talk soon." And then she disappeared back into the kitchen and sounds of pots and pans being pulled from shelves filled the café. That was Maggie, straight to the heart of business. And considering the big business of the day for Maggie was the wedding, Ellie forgave her.

"What's going on?" she asked as she put her laptop on the table and sank into a seat. "What are you guys up to?"

At first no one spoke, until Shirley said, "Well, to be honest, we're all in a tizzy about Ruth getting married in a few days and probably couldn't retain much that you want to teach us. So, we thought..."

She hesitated too long for Phil's liking and he blurted out, "We'd like to help you find your mom."

Ellie blinked; not sure she had heard them right. "Um..." She wiped her abruptly sweaty palm along her jeans. "Oh."

"I told you this wasn't a good idea," Ruth said, fixing Shirley with a stare. "This is none of our business, and Ellie should do this at her own pace. Not when we've put her on the spot."

"She might never do it, though," Norma said quietly from the seat next to her niece. "Ellie loved to start things when she was young, but there were more projects left unfinished than you can imagine."

"I'm sitting beside you, you know," Ellie said in a huff. She lowered her head and appeared to consider her aunt's words. The group was silent, allowing her to pull herself together. Finally, she straightened and glanced around at the waiting faces encircling the table. "Maybe we could take a brief look. To be honest, Aunt Norma is right. I finish things for other people, not so much for myself. But something about looking into my mother's past scares me."

"But if we're all here together," Tess said, "it won't be so hard."

"Sure," Lennie said. "We'll toss out ideas. We might come up with something helpful."

"And you have to admit, our ideas are getting better." Phil had almost inhaled a cookie and now brushed the crumbs from his fingers.

Ellie looked at her group and nodded. "Okay. Let's see what we find." The idea sent her heart racing, but the excitement overruled any fear at this point. People who loved her and wanted only the best for her, surrounded her. What could go wrong?

Norma pushed a box of tissue into the middle of the table. "Just in case we need them."

Ellie flipped open her laptop and waited for it to boot. "So, the only facts I have about my mom are her name and birthdate."

Norma fidgeted in her seat. "Actually, your mom once told me she was from Liverpool. I was pestering her something fierce because I was determined to figure out her accent."

"Mom didn't have an accent," Ellie said, looking at her aunt in confusion.

"She most certainly did!" Norma said. "And when she said Liverpool, it made sense. She tried to hide it, but it came out when she was tired."

"Why was she tired?" Ellie asked.

"I'm not sure, but I put it down to stress."

"About my dad or me?"

"No, never about you two," Norma hurried to assure her.

"And she never told you anything else about her past, her family, anything at all?"

Norma hesitated. Every face at that table was turned toward her, waiting for her answer. "She never said a word. And your dad always asked me not to pry. All he told me was that something happened when she was young, and she never wanted to talk about it. So, I let it go."

"You don't seem like a let it go kind of person," Shirley said, watching Norma's face. "You're a very take-charge kind of gal."

"My brother asked me not to pry, and I didn't." Norma shrugged. "I liked my privacy, so I understood and respected that."

"So, how will you start the search?" Ruth asked, leaning forward in keen interest.

"Well." Ellie tapped her pen against her chin and squinted, which was her usual deep thought activity. "Now that you've told me she came from Liverpool, and she was born in or around 1962, I'll start by looking at the FreeBMD site."

"What's that?" Phil asked, pen and notebook open and ready for information.

"They are a group in the UK who are transcribing the civil registrations for births, marriages and deaths in England and Wales. It's a pretty cool site, free, as the name suggests, and that's where I'm starting."

Her fingers flew and then she hit the enter key before scrolling through the entries that popped up. "Okay," she mumbled. "Here is the only Lisa Purvis. And it notes her mother's maiden name as being Wall. And there are no Elizabeth's, from which Lisa could be a nickname. And I never heard mom being called anything other than Lisa."

"It could also be Melissa," Ruth said.

"No." Norma shook her head. "Just Lisa."

"Okay," Ellie said, taking a breath. "So, we'll assume this is my mother. Let's find out if she had any siblings. One way is to use the same site and search for any other children with the Purvis last name, with the mother's maiden name as Wall, and I'll make the time frame for five years before and after my mom was born." She typed in the information.

"Well?" Shirley sat on the edge of her seat, arms on the table, leaning forward. "What does it say?"

"There's one entry for a boy named William, born two years before my mother."

"What else can you find?" Tess asked. "This is so exciting!"

"Now we'll check if the site has a record of my grandparents' marriage, so I can at least find their first names."

"But are those common names?" Lennie asked.

"I'm not sure." Ellie entered the information. "Obviously not common. There's only one match, and it's for two years before my uncle was born. The husband's name is Malcolm, and if I open the page, that will reveal the first name of the wife, which is Sylvia."

"So," Phil said, checking his notes. "Your mother is Lisa Purvis. Her mother is Sylvia Wall, and her husband is Malcolm Purvis. And your uncle was William. Is that correct?"

"Oh." Ellie jerked up, surprised by Phil's attention. "Yes, that sounds right. Now, with the date, volume and page numbers, plus the full names, I can order birth and marriage certificates for these people. Or I can see if they're in parish records through Ancestry. I can order right through Ancestry, though it's expensive, or I can go to the British General Register Office website and get it cheaper and faster. They guide you through the whole process, and have added a digital only option that's even cheaper than the normal orders. It's really simple, and I've used them for all my clients."

"But how do you know *this* is your mom's family? How can you be sure?" Norma asked.

"Why not check the newspapers for the family?" Phil suggested.

Ellie smiled. "Great next step, Phil."

"So," Ellie said as she started typing, "I'm going to use Newspapers.com again and enter my mom's name and Liverpool. I doubt anything will..."

Her face got increasingly pale as she read the article in front of her.

"Ellie?" Ruth said. "What's wrong?"

"Ellie?" Norma asked when her niece didn't respond.

"Okay," Ellie whispered to herself. "Okay."

"Did you find her?"

"I found them," Ellie said. "Her name is at the end of the article, along with her parents, but it's about her brother. He was convicted of murder and sentenced to twenty years. I skimmed it, but it said he testified that he killed this man to stop the man from hurting his sister."

"Your mother," Jeremy said quietly.

"I won't go through the process of finding his criminal records right now, because we did that once, but I will find it later. But I think I can say for sure that this is my family. The date is six months before my mother came over to Canada, or at least when my dad told me she arrived."

"Oh, lordy," Norma said under her breath, sure Ellie had found her family and worried about how it might affect her.

"Maybe you should stop, dear," Ruth said, noticing how Ellie's colour was rising.

"No, I want to explain these different ways of finding people to you," Ellie insisted. "I'm on to something here. So, we'll leave the brother alone for now, and try to find my mother coming over to Canada. My dad said they met in 1987, so she would have come before then." She took another look at the newspaper article. "And this all happened in 1984, so let's assume she came over during that period."

"Have you forgotten what you always say about assumptions!" Phil said, shaking his head at her.

"I know, I know," Ellie said. "But let's go with it for now. From previous research, I know Ancestry doesn't have any passenger lists that would equate to the time period she came over, so we'll have to find my parent's marriage certificate."

"You don't have that?" Shirley asked.

"No." Ellie shook her head. "When my parents died, it was quite a turbulent time. After the estate was settled, Aunt Jenna packed up their things and accidentally threw out all their documents with what she thought was junk."

"That's a shame," Norma muttered. "I didn't know that."

"I wasn't in any state to ask many questions right after they died," Ellie said. "And as the days, weeks, and months passed, I was just trying to survive without them."

"So, you really can't link this family to you until you get your parents' marriage certificate?" Jeremy asked.

"That's only if the names of their parents are on it," Ellie said. "Some certificates don't record them."

"Okay, wait," Norma said, holding up a hand. "You don't have to worry about this not being your family. It is. I'm sorry. Your dad told me the bare bones about what drove your mom from England, and it had to do with her brother being convicted of a crime. He didn't say what, but the evidence you have gathered points to this being accurate."

"Oh, my," Ruth whispered.

"Why the heck didn't you say that before?" Shirley asked.

"My brother told me this a long time ago, and I just remembered it now," Norma said.

"I find that hard to believe," Phil said.

Norma shrugged. "Sorry, guess I'm getting older."

"But why did she have to leave?" Ellie asked, ignoring the conversation around her, lost in thought as to the possibilities of her family history. "And are her parents still alive?"

"I can't answer your first question, but no, her parents aren't alive," Norma said.

The group was quiet, looking at each other, obviously feeling sorry for Ellie and not sure what to say to help her.

"Okay, well," Ellie said. "This is shocking, but it's great. Really."

Ruth patted her hand. "At least you've found your people."

"Yes, I have," Ellie nodded. "And everyone has skeletons in their closet. And if he was protecting my mother, it had to be something big."

"Have you got the wedding cake all figured out?" Ruth asked, changing the subject completely.

Ellie froze in shock for a minute, before her hand flew to her mouth. She jumped up and ran to the back of the Café. "Maggie! We have to talk!"

"Well done," Norma murmured to Ruth.

Chapter Twenty-Three

Ellie pushed the covers down and stretched her arms above her head. The sheets were rumpled from a restless sleep, but the sun peeking through the blinds made her smile.

It would be a good day for a wedding.

As thrilled as she was for the day ahead, her body refused to let her jump out of bed. The previous week had passed in a whirlwind with all the preparations she had agreed to take charge of, and now she needed to slow down. Add into the mix some restless nights after finding her mother's family, a sister of the bride trying to change plans at the last minute, and a groom so excited he could hardly eat, and Ellie had a lot to contend with.

A soft knock on her door made her hop out of bed and pull her housecoat on before opening the door. "Good morning," she whispered, not wanting to disturb the quiet of the morning with a loud voice.

"Good morning to you too," Quinn whispered back. "I've taken the beast for a walk and fed her. You obviously had a rough night."

She ran her hand through her tousled hair, embarrassed to be looking tired.

They headed down to the kitchen together. When Ellie saw the breakfast of eggs and bacon laid out on the table, she was so grateful she almost cried.

She threw her arms around Quinn's neck and hung on tight. "You are the best partner a girl could have," she mumbled into his shoulder.

He guided her to a chair before pouring her a glass of orange juice and sitting across from her. "I figured you'd be too excited to make something substantial. We both need to be on our toes this morning."

Ellie dug into her eggs and toast and gave him a brilliant smile. "This is exactly what I needed. I didn't even realize how hungry I was!" She shoved half of a piece of bacon into her mouth and grinned across at him.

"We have about an hour before the bride and her maid of honour turn up," Quinn said between bites of his own meal. "I think we should tidy and do a once over before changing."

Ellie turned to look at the clock and her eyes flew open wide. "Why did you let me sleep so late?"

"Because you were tired. We finished everything last night, and I needed time to get breakfast on the table."

She stopped eating and stared at him. How had she lucked into finding such a wonderful man? Maybe it was the whole approaching wedding vibe that was turning her to mush right now, but the two of them sitting at her kitchen table with the sun streaming through the windows seemed as close to perfect as her life could get.

Quinn caught her stare and raised an eyebrow. "What? Have I got food on my face or something?"

"No," she laughed and refocused on eating. "I don't think I've ever told you how grateful I am that you've come into my life."

"Not in so many words," he said. His meal finished, Quinn pushed his plate away and leaned on the table, a glass of juice cradled in his hands. "But it's safe to say I feel the same."

"And I can't thank you enough for all the help this week," Ellie said, catching his eye and holding it. "And putting your own work on hold to do so."

He reached out a hand to her, and she took it. "You know Ellie, I..."

A car pulled up outside and interrupted whatever he was going to say.

Ellie hurried to the door to see Shirley and Ruth easing out of their car and waving enthusiastically to her, huge smiles on their faces. This would be a happy day.

"I know, I know," Shirley said as she hurried to the porch. "We're very early, but we've been up since six, and figured we'd be more help here than getting all worked up at home."

Ruth joined her on the porch and Ellie opened the door to let them in.

"I'm sorry, dear," Ruth whispered to Ellie as Shirley walked into the kitchen to speak with Quinn. "She was so excited, and I had to get her out of the house."

"And you're not?" Ellie asked.

"More than you know." Ruth put her arm through Ellie's and gave her a squeeze. "But someone has to be the voice of calm."

"Have you spoken to Jeremy?" Ellie asked.

"Last night. He sounds like a kid!" Ruth laughed, delighted that the day was finally here. "I just want to make this official, and we'll have the rest of our lives to celebrate."

"So," Shirley said, standing with hands on hips in the middle of the kitchen as Quinn cleared away the breakfast dishes. "Where do we start?"

"Shirley," Quinn said, putting an arm around her shoulders and rocking her back and forth. It worked with his nephew, so it might calm a super excited Shirley. "Ellie and I finished all the work last night, but we'd love it if you would take some time to check things out in the barn and make sure everything is right."

"Of course, of course," Shirley pulled away from him, but he wouldn't let her go.

"But that's only *after* you and Ruth sit down and I make you some toast and tea," he said.

"Oh, we don't..." Shirley said.

"That would be lovely," Ruth said, sliding into a seat at the table, and taking in a deep breath. "We didn't feel like making anything this morning and we wouldn't want anyone to faint with hunger. Sit Shirley, let Ellie go get dressed and Quinn will make us that toast."

Shirley looked around the kitchen, as if something that needed to be done was waiting for her attention. Seeing nothing, she let out a breath and sank onto a chair. "Gosh," she said softly, "I had no idea how exhausting getting married was."

"That's why so many people help," Ellie said. "Now excuse me while I change. I figured we would set up your old bedroom, Ruth, as the final changing room before the ceremony. We can lounge in comfy clothes until then."

"Oh, yes, the clothes!" Shirley was up and out the front door before Ellie finished speaking.

"Let her go," Ruth said. "She needs to be doing something physical. She was never one to sit and ruminate when nervous."

"Shirley seems more nervous than you," Quinn said as he buttered the toast and brought it to the table. Jam was already out, and he returned once again with the tea.

"She is," Ruth said, reaching for a piece of toast. "Her life will change after today."

"So will yours," Ellie said.

"Yes, but it's going to be more difficult for her. I hope she'll get used to having a man around the house."

"I'll be back," Quinn said. He joined Shirley at the car and took the two clothing bags from her hands while Shirley grabbed the hat boxes and closed the door.

"You've got a good one there," Ruth said, looking from Quinn to Ellie.

"Don't I know it," Ellie said.

The sisters finished their breakfast quickly and the women retired to the bedroom to take the wedding apparel from their bags and place them carefully on hooks. Ellie took the sisters' hands and drew them close.

“I’m so glad this is happening, for both of you,” she said. “I’m thrilled that you’re getting married in your childhood home, Ruth. And Shirley, you being a part of this happy day will make it even more memorable.”

Ruth and Shirley looked at each other, smiled and pulled Ellie into a group hug.

“You’ve done wonders with the place, Ellie,” Shirley said. “And knowing we can come by anytime is a blessing. Now,” she stepped away and threw her shoulders back. “Let’s go check out the barn and see what magic you have rendered. But Ellie, do change, dear. Going about in your pajamas is not a good look.”

Ruth and Ellie snickered softly together, watching Shirley head outside in take charge mode.

***

Ellie had a quick shower, changed into jeans and a t-shirt, then joined Quinn, Ruth, and Shirley in the barn. Quinn stood by the door, Cali lying at his feet. He watched the sisters walk around, heads bent together, whispers and smiles telling him he and Ellie had done a good job.

“It’s lovely,” Ruth said.

“Quinn,” Shirley said. “Where are all your machines?”

He motioned to the two stalls in the back that were draped off. Shirley went over and pulled back the cloth, revealing the various tools Quinn used for his furniture making business.

“But the barn is so clean you could eat off the floor!” Shirley said in amazement. “How long did this take you?”

Quinn looked at Ellie and shrugged. “It took Ellie and I the afternoon. We work well together.”

“Obviously,” Ruth said. “I can’t thank you enough, both of you, for going to all this trouble for us.”

“You know we’d have it no other way,” Ellie said, taking a last critical walk around the room. The floor was indeed spotless. A long table ran along one side of the wall, covered in a floral tablecloth. Chairs were placed as if it were a church setting, facing the back with a small path between for the bride to walk down, and a lovely pale blue curtain hung at the front as a backdrop for the actual ceremony. All around the walls, above the windows, and across the curtain were strings of multicoloured faux flowers, borrowed from the town hall’s theatrical company. The windows themselves were sparkling clean and the morning sun was dancing through them, casting patterns across the floor.

“Now,” Ellie said with a quick clap of her hands as if to make herself focus. “Maggie should be here any minute and because it’s not hot, we’ll put the food out right away under screens. And I’ll go get all the paper plates and stuff, and then we wait.”

“Gosh, how I hate waiting!” Shirley moaned.

Chapter Twenty-Four

Shirley's wait was mercifully short. Maggie arrived ten minutes later with her boyfriend, Pete. Daphne was in the back, dressed smartly and ready to oversee the reception, while Maggie enjoyed the festivities as a guest. Maggie's car was loaded with goodies for the reception, and all hands gathered to transfer the food into the barn.

"Wow." Maggie placed a plate of sandwiches on the table and covered them with a screen, taking a minute to admire how the space had been transformed. "You guys did a great job."

"It's so country," Pete said, placing his platter next to Maggie's. "Last time I was here, there were huge machines and a lot of sawdust."

Quinn pointed to the back. "With the magic of stacking, everything is out of the way."

Shirley came in with a plate of pastries and hesitated. "Maggie, should we put these in the fridge?"

Maggie shook her head. "No, they'll do fine here. It's not hot enough to cause a problem, and everything will be eaten in a couple of hours, anyway! But the wedding cake has to go into the refrigerator. And I'll need help."

But it was Pete and Quinn who carefully removed the two-tiered cake from the car and slowly carried it into the house.

Ruth moved to catch a glimpse of it, but Maggie held her off. "Not yet, Ruth. I know most brides pick their own cakes, but you left it up to me, and I want it to be a surprise."

"Fair enough," Ruth said. Her cheeks rounded into apples of delight as she smiled at them all. "I can't believe everyone is doing this for us."

"Oh, tosh," Shirley said. "People hold you in high regard, Ruth, you know that. It's like we're all part of this amazing event together. Celebrating decades of love!"

"You're getting sentimental, Shirley," Ruth laughed. "How unlike you."

Shirley shrugged. "I guess all this love in the air is smoothing out my rough edges."

"Your *perceived* rough edges," Ruth said. She gave her sister a quick hug and then pulled her towards the house. "Let's go get dressed. People will be here anytime now."

They entered to find Ellie pulling items out of the refrigerator to make room for the cake.

"This way." Shirley steered Ruth away from the kitchen and led her to the back bedroom where their wedding clothes awaited.

***

"Okay." Ellie wheezed as she adjusted a shelf and motioned to the guys. "It should fit in now."

Together, Pete and Quinn lifted and then slid the cake into place, closing the door gently.

"That is an amazing cake," Pete said. "Maggie was up so early baking everything."

"Did you help?" Quinn asked.

"Ha!" Pete let out a barking laugh. "Help the Queen of Pastries? I think not. I was the supplier of ingredients, washer of dishes, and setter of timers. It's all I could handle, to be honest. That woman is a whirlwind; she had four things on the go at once. Oh, I helped with the sandwiches, though."

Ellie gave him a hug. "You're a peach, Cous. I can't thank you enough for this."

Quinn took a quick look at the clock. "Ellie, we better get dressed as well."

A car pulled up outside, and Ellie ran to the door. "It's the musicians."

Pete waved her off. "Go, get ready. I'll make sure they're settled. Where do you want them to set up?"

"Just inside the door, on the left. I made sure there's enough room for them. And tell them to pick chairs from the extra stack."

"Go, go." Pete pushed her away from the door and headed out to greet the musical entertainment.

"Right," Ellie said, but didn't move. She was lost in thought; positive something had escaped her meticulous list of items that needed to be done.

Quinn took her hand and pulled her up the stairs to the bedroom, where they would change. He had given his room to Ruth and Shirley as it was on the ground floor, and taken his clothes upstairs for the wedding.

"I'm looking forward to this," Quinn said as they entered the room. "I can't wait to see you in that dress."

Ellie shut the door behind them and let out a breath. "You've seen me in dresses before."

"Yes." Quinn said as he pulled his t-shirt off and slipped into his dress shirt, buttoning it in record time. "But not that one. I know how much effort you put into finding something special for this day. And the colours will highlight your blue eyes."

"My, but we're getting poetic this morning," Ellie said, loving he would notice such a thing.

"It's a big day and we might as well enjoy it." Quinn reached out and pulled her to him. "This is the first event like this that we've attended together."

Ellie wrapped her arms around his middle and leaned her head against his chest. There was something soothing about him being so tall, or was it that she was so short? The steady beat of his heart calmed her. "Not only are we attending a wedding together," Ellie said, looking up at him, "but we organized it together. We're a good team."

"We are indeed." He lowered his head and kissed her softly.

A car horn blared from outside and they jumped apart.

"Guests already and I'm not even dressed!" Ellie said. She looked around for her clothes.

Quinn quickly changed pants and headed for the door. "Not to worry. I'll greet them until you're ready. Maggie and Pete are there as well, and we'll get things sorted. Take a minute, my darling. All is well."

He gave her his signature lopsided grin, leaving her knees weak, then left. Ellie stood in the middle of the room, reliving his words—*My darling*. It had a nice ring to it. With a smile plastered to her face, Ellie slipped into her new blue dress, fought with her sandals and headed downstairs to check on the sisters.

She knocked on the bedroom door. It was thrown open seconds later by a flustered Shirley. The older woman gripped Ellie's arm and dragged her into the room, slamming the door behind her. "Help us!" Shirley's eyes were wide with panic.

"What's wrong?" Ellie looked over to Ruth, who sat quietly on the edge of the bed, two shoes in her hand.

"It's nothing, really," Ruth said.

Shirley took the shoes from Ruth and held them up. "They're not the same! She took two separate shoes from the cupboard this morning!"

Ellie stood back and inspected the shoes in Shirley's hands. "Well, they *are* different colours, but not glaringly so."

"I couldn't tell the difference in the dark this morning," Ruth said. "I'm sorry."

"What are you apologizing for?" Ellie asked in astonishment. "This isn't the end of the world."

"But they'll look funny," Shirley said, waving the shoes in the air.

Ellie took them from her and turned them over. "It's not like they're two for the same foot. Show me your dress, Ruth."

Ruth took the dress off the closet door and brought it over to Ellie. "I wanted nothing white, not at my age, but something upbeat, with colours that represent this time of year. I love the fall, and I think all these browns and golds are beautiful."

"They are," Ellie said. "And look at this." She brought the shoes close to the dress and they could all see that each shoe's colour was duplicated in the dress. "You'll start a trend, Ruth."

Ruth smiled and finished taking the plastic covering off her dress. "Then that's that. Let's get dressed, Shirley. I can hear people arriving and I don't want to be late to my own wedding!"

Shirley shook her head, as if realizing that the shoes really weren't that big a deal.

***

Ellie left the women to finish dressing and stepped out onto the porch in time to see Quinn wave at her from her Aunt Norma's car as he drove past. He was playing valet today to make everyone's life a bit easier.

Norma waved at her from the entrance to the barn, Virginia at her side. Together they called out, "Hello there!"

Ellie went up for a hug and walked into the barn with them. "This is a delightful surprise, Virginia. It's good to see you again."

"Well, I told Norma I would visit and this seemed like a good time. Ruth and Jeremy were very kind in inviting me."

"Hello, hello," called Tess from the door. She looked lovely in a pale blue knee length dress. Lennie and Phil were wearing suits and ties. Doreen brought up the rear in a pink pantsuit.

"Where should I park?" Lennie asked, his keys jingling in his hand.

"Leave that to me." Quinn had just returned. He took the keys, pivoted, and headed back out.

"My goodness, how lovely," Tess whispered as she looked around the barn. "Let's go mingle."

Ellie stood planted by the door, taking a calming breath, loving the fact so many people were here to share Ruth and Jeremy's ceremony.

A handful of people had already taken seats, most of them strangers to Ellie. They must be Jeremy's friends. They all turned and waved.

Quinn walked in behind Ellie and whispered in her ear. "Friends from the retirement home. The lady in pink wants to hire me for something, so don't leave me alone with her."

Ellie laughed and covered it with a cough. One musician was playing his cello and the other was tuning his violin. They were both dressed in black suits but looked to be about twelve years old.

"Very fancy," Norma said, nodding at the duo.

"Students from the high school," Ellie said. "They're quite good. I believe our officiant has arrived."

Mayor Savard strode towards them, hands outstretched, a huge smile on his face. "I am so honored to be asked to preside today."

"Ruth has a soft spot for you, Mayor Savard," Ellie said, shaking his hand and ushering him into the barn.

"I didn't know a mayor could marry people," Virginia said.

"You can designate anyone to do so in a civil marriage," Ellie explained. "But the person can only do so for this marriage, on this precise day. At least that's the rules for Quebec."

Mayor Savard looked at his watch and then at Ellie. "Are we still on for eleven o'clock?"

"Yes, we are," Ellie said. Most of the small party of family and friends were present, but Jeremy and his immediate family had yet to arrive. "I'll check on the bride, and as soon as Jeremy gets here, we can start."

Mayor Savard nodded and headed inside, speaking to the groups of people already seated.

"Where is Jeremy?" Quinn asked, a touch of nervousness in his voice. "I thought he'd be here early."

"He's still got time," Ellie assured him, double checking her watch. It was now five past eleven. "I'm sure he'll be here any minute."

Norma poked her arm and pointed at the house. "Shirley is trying to get your attention."

And indeed, Shirley was at the front door, both hands waving at her to come inside.

Ellie took a deep breath and hurried to the house. "What's wrong?" she asked Shirley as she reached her.

"Come quick," Shirley headed to the bedroom. "Ruth saw the time and is having a meltdown."

Chapter Twenty-Five

Ellie didn't believe for a minute that Ruth was the type of woman to have a meltdown, but it *was* true Ruth had never been married before, and she *was* tired.

But the woman who was standing by the window in the bedroom was not in distress in any visible way. Ruth turned to them as Shirley bustled through the door, Ellie at her heels. "What's wrong?" Ruth asked.

"Nothing," Ellie answered, somewhat confused. She turned to Shirley with a questioning look.

"Well, he's not here yet, is he?" Shirley demanded, wringing her hands.

Ruth reached out and quieted Shirley's fidgeting. "At our age," she said, "we can't do everything right on the dot. He'll be here."

Shirley looked at her watch. "But it's..."

"Shirley," Ellie said loudly, startling them both. "Can you get Ruth a glass of water please?"

"Yes, yes, of course." Shirley was out the door as fast as she could.

"Oh, thank you, dear," Ruth said with a weary smile. She lowered herself onto the bed and sighed. "I'm not even married yet and I'm exhausted!"

Ellie sat beside her and took her hand. "I don't remember much about my wedding day, sadly. I'm told I had a great time. But I was so nervous, so worried about every little thing, that I didn't pay attention to what was important."

"Oh, I'm fully aware of everything," Ruth said. "I'm a little worried about Jeremy."

"They're here!" Shirley's shout was joyous. She burst into the room, glass in hand, water dripping down the sides of it. "The car just pulled in and the guys are getting out and..."

"Shush, Shirley," Ruth said. "Please. You're making me nervous."

"Right. Sorry." Shirley held out the glass to her sister and Ruth gratefully took a few sips before putting it on the bedside table.

Ellie stood up and went to the door. "I'm going to make sure everything is settled and people are in their places, then I'll be back. It might take a couple of minutes, so don't fret. And Ruth?"

Ruth looked at her.

"You look lovely."

***

Ellie dashed outside to see Quinn once again guiding a car down the driveway. He gave her a huge grin and jaunty wave.

Members of Jeremy's family were standing outside the barn, looking around themselves with obvious admiration. When he saw her, Jeremy hurried over and gave Ellie a hug.

"This is so kind of you, Ellie," he said breathlessly. "What a wonderful setting. Where's Ruthie?"

"You'll see her when she walks down the aisle, and not a minute before," Ellie teased him.

"And I'm so sorry we're late," Jeremy said.

Sam shook Ellie's hand before introducing her to his family. He motioned to a lady dressed in a light pink dress and matching coat. "My patient wife, Caroline." Looking down at his two children in their Sunday best, he ruffled the hair on his son's head. "This is Jason." His son tugged at his tie every couple of minutes.

"And this lovely lady is Patricia." His daughter smiled shyly and then twirled in her flouncy dress.

"Lovely to meet you all," Ellie shook Caroline's hand.

"Dad had a bit of trouble picking the right tie," Sam said in way of explanation for their tardiness.

"He only had three!" Jason said, shaking his head.

"Right," Caroline took the hand of each child. "Let's go in and get seated so your grandfather can get married. He's waited long enough."

They disappeared into the barn with Sam staying with his father. Sam suggested, "I guess we should go and take our places. If Ruth is as nervous as you, I think it's best not to prolong it."

"Yes, yes," Jeremy agreed, searching his pant pocket and pulling out a piece of paper. "My vows," he said, holding the worn-thin paper up.

After Jeremy and Sam entered the barn, Ellie checked to make sure everyone was in place, and gave Mayor Savard a nod.

Quinn met her outside. "Everything ready?"

"Almost," Ellie said. "When you see us coming, could you let the musicians know to start the wedding procession song, please?"

"Sure."

With one last glance around, she hurried back to the house to get the bride.

***

When Ellie walked into the bedroom, Shirley was fussing with Ruth's beige veil, affixing it to her hair with tiny pins, and arranging it tenderly around her sister's shoulders, a dreamy expression on her face.

"I don't know why I need a veil," Ruth murmured.

"Oh, let me have this, Ruth, please," Shirley pleaded. "I'll never get married, and I've always imagined you in white. So, this will have to do."

"It's very lovely, Ruth," Ellie said. The woman before her had a glow about her. Ruth's eyes were sparkling and a sense of calm had descended.

"It is," Ruth agreed. "Thank you, Shirley. You're the best sister a girl could ask for."

"I'm not and you know it," Shirley whispered. She wiped some tears from her eyes and turned to Ellie. "So, is everyone in place? Did Jeremy finally turn up?"

"Everyone is waiting for the bride and Jeremy is terribly nervous," Ellie said.

"Oh, that poor man," Ruth said, leading the way from the room. "Let's put him out of his misery."

As they stepped out on the porch, the music started. Ruth staggered to a stop.

"Oh, my," she said. "I've heard that song so often during my life, but this time it's for me!"

"Are we ready?" Shirley asked her softly, holding out her arm. With no father to give her away, Ruth had asked Shirley not only to be her Maid of Honour, but also to walk her down the aisle. Shirley took both roles very seriously.

Ruth laid her hand on Shirley's arm and they strode into the barn.

As they walked down the aisle, all heads turned to them. Ruth gripped Shirley tighter. "I didn't think everyone would come!" she whispered without moving her lips.

Shirley's only response was a return squeeze, as they had reached the front where Jeremy stood. His eyes were damp and his smile was wide.

Quinn moved around the barn slowly, taking pictures of all the guests. Now he found himself slightly behind Mayor Savard, in the perfect position to capture Ruth and Shirley coming up the aisle.

Jeremy held out his hands to Ruth and she quickly passed her bouquet to her sister before placing her hands in Jeremy's. Sam stood behind him. He gave Ruth a quick nod and a wink.

"Dearly beloved," Mayor Savard said. "I welcome you all here today to witness the marriage of Ruth Cotter and Jeremy Butler. Being a civil union, they have asked that they only read their vows before I pronounce them husband and wife."

Jeremy turned to the small crowd. "We didn't want to keep you, and gosh, we've waited a long time for this!"

After the laughing died down, Jeremy let go of Ruth's hands to take his piece of paper from his pocket. He opened it, pushed his glasses up his nose, and held out his hand again. Ruth took it.

"Ruthie." His voice crackled, so he coughed and started again. "Ruthie. You were the first love of my life. Your letters through the war got me through those horrible months, and finding you again after all this time has completed my circle of life. While we missed out on a lot of things a married couple would experience, I never thought I'd be given this second chance to spend the best days of my life with you." He looked up from his paper and went rogue. "And they *will* be the best days. You have always been in my heart and I will spend the rest of our lives making sure you know how much you are loved and cherished."

He kissed her hand and pulled his handkerchief from his pocket, passing it to her. "I love you."

The sound of someone blowing their nose caught everyone's attention. Phil wiped his eyes and stuffed his tissue back in his pocket. He refused to meet anyone's gaze. Shirley winked at him and his chin wobbled.

Ruth wiped her eyes too, clutching the cloth he'd given her in one hand while she reached out the other to Jeremy. "We can never go back, only forward. What may have been will never be known, but what will be is for us to choose. You have always been the measure by which I make decisions. I've not found anyone who brought calm and peace to me as you have. We will be a force to be reckoned with, you and I, Jeremy Butler, because our love will blow those Hollywood movies out of the water!"

The guests started clapping and Doreen called out. "You show them, Ruth!"

Quinn had stepped into the aisle and was hunkered down on one knee. He knew what was coming and was determined to get the perfect pictures.

Sam whispered in his father's ear. Jeremy stuck his hand in his pocket and brought out a gold band. He held it out and took Ruth's hand in his, gently sliding the ring up her finger.

Shirley passed something to Ruth, and Ruth then repeated the gesture with Jeremy. They held each others hands, rings touching as Mayor Savard threw back his shoulders and gazed out at the wedding party.

"And now, by the powers vested in me for this one and only time, I hereby pronounce you husband and wife. You may kiss the..."

But Jeremy was way ahead of him. He took Ruth's shoulders and leaned in for a Hollywood worthy sweet kiss.

Everyone was on their feet as the newlyweds turned to their friends and family. The music started and everyone cheered.

Quinn's final ceremony picture would rest on their mantel for the rest of their lives. Arms around each other, beaming smiles, Ruth and Jeremy looked decades younger than anyone could imagine.

"It's time to eat!" Jeremy called out, his arm firmly around his wife. "Let's get this party started!"

Chapter Twenty-Six

Ellie brought small tables from the back and placed them at intervals along the wall. She directed Pete and others to move the chairs from their previous positions and place them at the various tables so people could sit and eat.

Quinn entered with a huge bowl of punch and centered it in the middle of the food table, while Ellie made sure there were enough plates and cups for all.

"Dig in, everyone," Ellie announced to the group.

It took a while for everyone to get their meals, because each one had gone to give Ruth and Jeremy a hug and wish them well.

"No beer?" Phil asked, as he filled his plate with delicate sandwiches.

"We didn't want anyone drunk this early in the day," Jeremy said. "We'll have to amend that at a later date."

"You never did get a stag party," Lennie said as he stepped up with his paper plate.

"Not much of a party when we'd all be in bed at nine!" Jeremy laughed.

"Speak for yourself," Phil said. "I've been managing nine thirty for years." At that moment, a loud grumble came from his stomach.

"Phil!" Shirley said as she stepped beside him at the table. "You need to feed that machine of yours. Did you not have breakfast?"

"I must confess that when I heard Maggie was catering, I wanted to have enough room to try everything."

"Wait till you see the wedding cake," Daphne said from her post behind the table. She handed out some napkins. "Will you have some punch?"

Phil looked at his plate, which was clutched in both hands. "I don't know how..."

"That's my job," Ellie said as she motioned for Daphne to fill a few cups. "Let's get you a seat. Shirley, you coming?"

Shirley had stopped and was looking at the joy on the faces of her sister and new brother-in-law. "Yes." She followed Ellie and Phil to a table where they gratefully placed their plates down and sank into their seats.

The musicians played softly in the corner while the guests enjoyed Maggie's amazing food. Ellie watched over the event, gauging the pace of the meal. When she saw most guests seemed to have had their fill, she nodded to Quinn and Pete to follow her into the house.

A few minutes later, they were back at the entrance to the barn and Ellie was clapping her hands to get everyone's attention.

"I think everyone has finished the main meal, so we'd like to present the new couple with a one-of-a-kind Maggie Williams creation."

Maggie had pulled one table into the middle of the room where the guys gently set down the cake. Ellie let a relieved sigh escape her lips, then motioned the bride and groom forward. Intrigued, Ruth and Jeremy approached with anticipation. Atop the cake were the bride and groom, each one age appropriate, and they looked very similar to Ruth and Jeremy.

"Would you look at that!" Ruth said. "Jeremy, it's us!"

Jeremy peered closer, then over at Maggie. "Is this your doing?"

Maggie nodded. "I've taken a few classes on how to create figures and different things for cakes. I'm upping my skill set."

"Come on, everyone," Norma said, getting up from her seat and heading to the table. "Let's look at this before they slice and dice it."

Quinn had already taken photos in the kitchen, and now walked around the edge of the barn, taking candid photos of everyone as they admired the cake.

"It's time for the cake picture!" Tess said. "Who's got the knife?"

Maggie took a long knife from beneath a napkin. It had a red ribbon tied to the handle. She handed it to Jeremy. "I believe you are both supposed to hold this and make the first cut."

Guests made way for Quinn to capture that perfect shot.

Ruth, who had not stopped smiling since she'd walked into the barn, put her hand atop Jeremy's and together they cut the first slice. Jeremy put it on a plate and handed it to Ruth. She picked up two forks and led him to their table at the front, and sat down beside him.

As they ate, they watched Maggie cut up slices for everyone else, their expressions glowing.

"Maggie!" Ruth said. "This is the most delicious cake I've ever eaten. And I'm not saying that because it's my wedding cake."

"I hope you're adding this to your business," Doreen said, putting a last piece in her mouth and eyeing the cake still in place on the table. "This would work amazing as cupcakes as well."

"I hope we're getting some to take with us," Jeremy said, wiping his mouth with his napkin.

"I'll make sure there's some waiting for you when you get back," Shirley assured him. "And I've always wanted a brother!" The last comment was so spontaneous Shirley looked shocked at herself.

"He's moving in with us," Ruth announced to the group.

"But don't worry," Jeremy said to his retirement home friends. "I will be back to visit."

"And what are you doing for your honeymoon?" Tess asked as everyone made quick work of their pieces of cake.

"Jeremy is taking me to the Fairmont Chateau Montebello for a two-night stay," Ruth said, her cheeks turning pink.

"That's where he proposed!" Norma said. "What a brilliant idea."

"And expensive," Phil said under his breath.

"Honestly, Phil," Jeremy said with a laugh. "We're old. Why not spend our money on something that will bring us joy? Especially now!"

"And I'm taking a vacation too," Shirley piped up, never one to be left out of any situation. "I'm staying with Ellie and Quinn for a couple of days."

Before anymore conversation could arise, Ellie nodded at the musicians, who started playing more upbeat music. Dancing music.

"If everyone agrees, it's time for our newlyweds to have a first dance before we all hit the floor," Shirley announced. "Something slower." She raised an eyebrow at the musicians and they nodded.

Everyone helped move the table from the center of the floor, and Ruth and Jeremy took their places of honour in the middle of their friends.

The first strands of "Only You" came from the violin, and Ruth and Jeremy started dancing. They looked like they had been together all their lives, each in step, gliding together in perfect unison.

"Okay," Jeremy said over his shoulder, "everybody join in. We won't last long!"

Other couples stepped onto the floor and Quinn pulled Ellie into his arms. They fit perfectly, but before they knew it, the song was over. Some people returned to their seats while others walked around to chat.

Jeremy introduced his retirement home friends to the group, and many funny stories were told. The barn was filled with laughter. Compliments were given to Maggie for the wedding feast she had prepared, and Ruth's foot kept tapping in time to the music.

Ellie found a moment to find her aunt alone by the punch bowl. "It's great to see Virginia here."

"Yes, she's staying with me for a few days," Norma said before taking a sip of the punch. "She's going to talk to Sara at the Tiny House Haven and see if something might be available."

"That would be great," Ellie said. She gave her aunt a side glance. "So, what did Virginia mean about you wanting to be a spy?"

"You caught that, did you?"

"Well?"

"I'm not at liberty to discuss it, dear."

Ruth and Jeremy grabbed everyone's attention as they stood in the door to the barn.

"Thank you all for this wonderful day," Jeremy said. "But Ruthie and I are about to head out in our chariot for our honeymoon."

"Since Sam is kindly driving us there, we'll probably sleep on the way!" Ruth joked. "But thank you all for sharing this day with us. We will see you when we get back."

"Pace yourselves!" Lennie said, and was immediately elbowed in the ribs by Tess.

"Don't forget the bouquet," Doreen called out to Ruth. She took it from the table where Ruth had placed it and handed it to the bride. "Now, turn around and toss it over your head. Whoever catches it is getting married next!"

The men in the group hurried to the sides of the bar, out of the way of the possibility of catching the flowers. All except for Phil. With a shrug, he stood behind all the women, sure he wouldn't catch it, but up for a challenge.

Ruth turned her back to them, gripped the bouquet tight and gave a mighty toss up and over her head.

There was silence, and then Ruth turned around.

Ellie stood in the middle of the floor with the bouquet in one hand and a look of astonishment on her face.

THE END

About the Author

Beth Farrar has been writing stories since her parents handed her a library card. Her imagination was sparked. Encouragement from English teachers set her on a serious path of learning the craft.

From writing TV scripts to full length movies for pleasure and practice, she developed her writing skills by exploring various mediums. Filling notebooks with ideas, sketching characters and locations, and inventing sticky situations for characters to survive, is Beth's happy place (besides walking in cemeteries, but that's another story).

For fifteen years Beth wrote a monthly column, Living Country, in her local English language newspaper, Main Street, sharing interesting observations of living and raising her three sons in the country with her husband. Having always loved genealogy, Beth melded two of her passions together and created the Ellie McLellan Genealogy Mystery series.

For tips and tricks on how to write your own personal history story, head over to Beth Farrar – Author on Facebook for more information. Or visit her website bethfarrar.com and join her newsletter to get a free Oral History Questions booklet to start your journey writing your own personal story.

Afterword

Would you like to write your own personal story? Head over to my Instagram page, or my Facebook site at "Beth Farrar – Author". You'll find more tips about how to start putting together your own life story. And join my newsletter at bethfarrar.com.

The seniors in Ellie's genealogy group learned a couple of things during this story that you can apply to your own journey.

1. **Newspapers.com** $ – The events that old newspapers documented can fill in a lot of holes in your research. Use maiden and married names for women, leave the dates open, narrow down the locale. I found my father in the death notice of another relative.

2. **Findagrave.com** $ – You may get lucky and find not only the records for an ancestor, but also a picture of the tombstone. There may also be a brief family tree included in the entry.

3. **Oldbaileyonline.org** – This free site is priceless if you have ancestors who lived in London. Instructions for using the site are great, you get to read the actual record of the trial, and find out what their sentence was.

4. **FreeBMD.org.uk** – This can find an ancestor, discover a maiden name, and give you the Volume and Page numbers to help order certificates.

Acknowledgements

There are a few people I'd like to give a fist bump to. First is my editor, Ronnie Roberts, who comes through for me every time, and on time. She answers all my questions and makes suggestions that fit perfectly with what I've written.

My main reader, Teresa O'Neil, who thankfully tells me how much she likes something or feels it needs work. Your honesty is priceless and the fact that you word the comments so politely, makes it easier to hear.

Daphne Petersen and her amazing ability to find those little niggly bits that I'm SURE we had caught! You've kept me from having to answer to readers who like to point out mistakes.

Liam, Connar and Devlin, my cheerleaders, who get as excited as I do when anything good happens.

And my wonderful hubby, who encourages me every day in fulfilling my dream. Your behind the scenes help keeps me going on those days when I'm sure the ideas have dried up.

Family Christmas-Book 5

Family feuds can be triggered by different factors, including misunderstandings, pride, greed, and envy.

This Christmas season, genealogist Ellie McLellan is put in charge of organizing the Percyville holiday festivities. Together with her dwindling senior genealogist group, she endeavors to plan an exceptional event for the town.

But when a family feud is unexpectedly thrust upon her, she must find a Percyville treasure before the last generation renews the feud or destroys the town's Christmas tradition.

Will the elders of the community have the clues Ellie needs to solve this mystery?

Will she recover the item before it is stolen a second time and lost forever?

Printed in Great Britain
by Amazon

60766273R00111